Summer Cool

Summer Cool
A Jack Paine Mystery

Al Sarrantonio

Walker and Company
New York

First published in the United States of America in 1993
by Walker Publishing Company, Inc.

Published simultaneously in Canada by Thomas Allen & Son
Canada, Limited, Markham, Ontario

Library of Congress Cataloging-in-Publication Data
Sarrantonio, Al
Summer cool / Al Sarrantonio.
p.   cm.
"A Jack Paine mystery."
ISBN 0-8027-3235-6
I. Title.
PS3569.A73S86   1993
813'.54—dc20   92-38253
CIP

Printed in the United States of America
2 4 6 8 10 9 7 5 3 1

For Gorman,
Lansdale,
and Raisor:
a few good men.

When summer cool
and winter warm
Do change the world again . . .

—*William Drayden*

Summer Cool

$\triangledown$

1

Paine ignored the ringing phone.

The chilled frost on his iced tea glass hadn't had time to melt and put a water stain on the redwood bench on which it rested. His web-backed lounger was finally at the right position for reading the fat political novel that lay unopened next to the iced tea. If he wished, he could put on the sunglasses that rested on top of the book, and gaze out from the shade of his tree through the early afternoon glare across the small lake to see if any largemouth bass were jumping at flies from under their lily pads. His fishing pole lay within reach, fixed with the Jitterbug lure that had netted him nine fish in two days—eight of them the previous evening alone as the sun settled leisurely into the coolness of the trees, and the bass, warmed after a day of ninety-degree heat, had decided to jump at anything that moved on the water.

Behind him, the tape deck had auto-reversed, and the second side of the Keith Jarrett recording was beginning, carrying Paine back into the improvisational piano fugue the first side had begun.

The telephone continued to ring.

"Screw it," Paine said out loud, settling back into the perfect curve of the lounge chair, his hand falling to lift the glass of iced tea to his mouth.

There were only a few people who might call him, and none of them would do it. They knew why he was here and they knew he didn't want to be disturbed. They knew how hard he had worked the past year, especially the past month, in the middle of the hottest summer in thirty-four years, and they knew how much he wanted to be alone, to fish and read and listen to music during the day, and go out to the big white dome holding the twelve-inch telescope at night, the one his dad and brother and he had built so long ago, and look at the stars and believe that, in their cool serenity, their cold majesty, their distance from small problems, human concerns, the cares of any one life, they could continue to heal him. Whoever might call him would know what it meant for him to be here, and would not call him. It must be a wrong number.

The ringing continued.

He pushed the sunglasses aside and lifted the book, fingering the cover without opening it.

"Shit," he said.

He could let it ring until whoever it was got tired and hung up. But the carefully constructed mood he had worked on all morning was broken, Jarrett's delicate piano subsumed by sharp phone sounds, the iced tea beginning to stain the redwood, the mosquitoes in the hot of the day beginning to drift off the lake to hover like annoying darts around him. He put the book down, no longer wanting to start it.

Somewhere inside him, anger stirred.

The phone rang, and now he wanted to get up and answer it and find out which aluminum siding salesman was calling, or what water softener company, or which wrong number. He would find out, politely asking who he was speaking to and where they were located, and then he would get in his car and take a ride over there, and punch the caller out.

But that would mean getting out of the chair, which still cradled him, and it would mean walking out of the shade of the tree into the burning sun to get to the house. There was still a remnant of his anticipated afternoon left, and as he looked at Gore Vidal's picture on the back of his book he felt a renewed longing to open it and lose himself in it. There were three other books back in the house to read, another week of fishing and sleep and no television and no world.

He should have pulled the phone out of the wall the first night he got up here.

"*Shit,*" he said again, getting up from his lounge chair and making the short, hot walk to the house. Sweat immediately beaded the back of his neck at the slight exertion.

He grabbed the phone from its cradle and said, "Jack Paine."

"Thank God."

It was someone he knew. But he could not place the voice—it sounded familiar but the near hysteria in it didn't.

"Who—"

"Jack, it's Terry Petty."

There was still no recognition. He knew the name but the voice did not connect to it. There was a gap between expectation and reality: The mailman seen out of uniform in the grocery store will trigger recognition but no identification.

Terry Petty . . . His brain filled the gap, made the connection, a second before she spoke again in his silence.

Terry Petty. Bobby's wife.

"Terry, what's wrong?"

"I . . . a lot."

He had never heard her like this, and that was where the gap had been; she had always been someone who was there and solid, a cop's wife, a mother of two with her head screwed on straight.

"One of the kids?"

She fought a small battle with herself and a measure of calm won. "It's Bobby."

An image flashed through Paine's head—Bob Petty on the ground, a shotgun wound leaking his life onto the sidewalk, into the gutter somewhere, running footsteps away from him. . . .

"What happened, Terry?"

"He's not dead." She had read his voice, and the way she had said it scared him more because it told him that this was something worse than that.

"Come on, Terry, say it."

"He . . . he's gone."

"What do you mean?"

"He's disappeared, Jack. He went out last night and he didn't come back."

"Terry," Paine said delicately, "do you think maybe he went on a bender or something, had a couple of drinks too many and slept it off in the back of some bar? It wouldn't be the first—"

"Goddamn it, Jack!"

He was quiet. In the background he heard a child's voice, and Terry paused, trying not to sob, telling one of her daughters to go away. Paine heard the daughter, Melissa it sounded like, fourteen years old, protest and tell Terry she was worried about her. Terry screamed at her to get out and the girl, sobbing, retreated.

"Listen to me, Jack," she said, calmer. "He was acting edgy after he got home last night, but it wasn't anything he wanted to talk about. At nine-thirty he said he was going out to get some ice cream for the kids. About eleven I started to get worried. I called the deli he would have gone to. They never saw him. So I called Coleman and told him what happened. He said the same thing you did, but said they'd keep their eyes open for him. You know what I was thinking, a robbery, he pulls out his revolver, something like that. I was *worried*, Jack. I made sure the kids were in bed and then I lay down on the couch to wait. I fell asleep. When I woke up the phone was ringing. It was four in the morning. When I picked it up—" She hesitated, fighting herself again.

"Come on, Terry."

"It was Bobby, Jack. I've never heard him talk to me like that before. Never. He started cursing at me. Then he told me he'd been with another woman. He sounded drunk, so I tried to calm him down. But he just kept going into me, Jack. How bad a mother I was, what a rotten life he'd had with me. Things he'd never said before, even when we had our worst fights. It was him talking, Jack, but I can't believe it was him. He said he was sick of being a cop, sick of me and the kids and everything else. He said he was with this other woman and that he was going away. He said . . ." She sobbed, then regained herself. "He said if I ever came near him he'd kill me and the kids! My God, Jack, he *loves* the girls! He'd never hurt them. I *know* Bobby, I know everything about him and know he wouldn't really mean those things—he told me he never loved me, Jack! *God, what am I going to do?*"

She wept, and as this strong woman tried to bring herself under control for him Paine thought about how well he too knew Bob Petty.

"Meet me at my office in an hour," he said.

Paine turned off the tape deck on his way through the house to the car.

Outside under the sun, the frost on the iced tea was gone. The tea began to get warm. The book went unread, and the fish weren't caught, and Paine's empty lounge chair listened to his car as it took him away from all hope of rest.

2

Yonkers gets as hot as the next place in the summer. But this summer was hotter than most. Con Edison was running at three brownouts a week, and there had already been one blackout that had threatened to turn into an East Coast disaster, saved at the last minute, so the power authority had claimed, by its nuclear turbine up the Hudson River near Peekskill named Big Alice. None of the papers had believed it, and very few of the people who read papers, and two days later, when Big Alice shut itself down, not to be reactivated until Christmas by Con Edison estimates, well, everybody turned on their air conditioners and prayed.

Paine had prayed, and his air conditioner had gone out instead of the power, and the hotbox his landlord tried to tell him was an office suite was a hotbox and nothing more. Two fans blew humid top-story air at each other, and in between them Paine sweated, and though Terry Petty sweated she was unaware of the weather.

She had been waiting for him outside his office. She had calmed down. She was more like the Terry he knew: petite, quiet in dress and manner, a cop's wife, which meant that the surface was deceptive. Underneath the quiet exterior, behind the green eyes, she was a rock; she had raised two girls and one husband, most times with calm, with fire when needed. She was a woman Paine had often openly admired, and Petty had never contradicted Paine's compliments—and Petty had never kept his mouth shut about anything he felt.

"I'm sorry for the way I acted on the phone, Jack," she

said. "And I'm sorry I dragged you away from your vacation—"

"We've known each other too long for bullshit, Terry," he said, gently. He had begun by playing with a pencil on his desk, quickly graduating to the letter opener. Nearly a week's worth of unopened mail, what he could see of it bills, was stacked roughly on the edge of the desk where he had thrown it after gathering it up from the inside of the letter slot. "I think the best thing is to go at this straight, just like Bobby would." Paine pushed himself back in his chair, continuing to finger the letter opener. "I don't mean to sound like a jerk, but I think that maybe you're being a hysterical wife."

Her face reddened, as he knew it would. She had more Irish blood in her than Petty, and when riled she could be more of a marine than her ex-marine husband ever could.

"Bullshit, Jack. Do you think I would have bothered you for something stupid?"

Paine continued to play devil's advocate. "I still think he's gone undercover for some reason."

She was growing angrier. "I thought of that. It was possible, the thing he was working on. We had a code worked out between us, if that ever happened. He would always be able to tell me if he was undercover, or couldn't talk. He even used it once."

"What was the code?"

"He'd talk about the girls, and say, 'I think we should have one birthday party for the two of them.' Their birthdays are six months apart."

"You're sure he didn't use it this time?"

"He didn't use it. He said *horrible* things about the girls."

Paine took a long breath. "I'm sorry, Terry, but I've got to ask you these things. Were you having any marital trouble?"

"No."

"Do you think he might have been seeing another woman?"

She hesitated in silence. "I thought of that, he said he was with one."

"Is it possible?"

She took a long breath, as if resigning herself to the con-
clusion she had come to. "It's possible."

He hated pushing her. "Has there ever been anything like
that?"

Again she hesitated. Paine thought she might be measur-
ing the line where friendship ended and enmity began. Paine
was about to say gently that maybe she should get someone
else to help her when she nodded. "Once. A long time ago."

"How long?"

"Eight years ago. Just around the time we moved to Yonkers from the Bronx. It was somebody he met on a case he
was working on."

"How long did it last?"

"Four months. He told me about it when it was over."

She looked up at Paine. There was a kind of pleading in
her face. "He *cried* when he told me about it, Jack. He said
it had happened and he'd felt guilty through the whole thing
and he never wanted to feel guilty again. He said he'd never
stopped loving me; it was just after Mary was born and everything had changed in the house with the baby, and we
weren't . . ." she bit her lip, not wanting to say anymore to
him. "We weren't *doing* it, Jack. I was tired from the baby, it
was a hard birth, the doctor said I had to rest—*dammit, Jack,
that's not what this is!*"

He stared at her levelly until the flush receded from her
face and then he asked, softly and evenly, "Is that what you
believe, or is it what you want to believe?"

Her eyes were just as steady on his. "It's what I believe,
Jack. I don't think he'd do that to his family."

Paine had been jabbing himself in the palm with the letter
opener. He put it down on the desk next to the bills. "For
what it's worth, I don't think he'd do that to you, either. But
unfortunately what I believe and what you believe doesn't
mean anything. If it makes you feel any better, Bobby told
me all about that affair of his; we got drunk one night and
he spilled it out. Nobody in the department knew about it.
It sounded like it tore him up inside. But the thing I'm

getting at is that sometimes people have things inside them they don't let anybody see—not their wives, not their friends. If I had to put money on it I'd put it all on Bobby not being one of those people. But I've got to be honest with you, Terry, I might lose my money. Because it's just a fact that most people who disappear do it because they want to."

A little bit of her crumbled inside. He saw it happen, and he wanted very badly to go back and say it another way, so that she would stay whole. But he knew that no matter how he said it, the same thing would happen, because she had had a world built around her, and all the blocks had suddenly been yanked out of the foundation, and there was no way that world was going to look the same after the rest of the building fell into place.

"Did you talk to Coleman today?" Paine said. He spoke without force, afraid that if his voice were any louder her building might collapse completely.

"I called him this morning. He told me that Bobby had called and told *him* to go to hell."

"Has Bobby called anyone else?"

"Nobody else at the station. None of his other friends. We were supposed to go down to the Bronx on Saturday for a barbecue a few of his old NYPD buddies put together, but he didn't call any of them. I tried his brother in Albany, too, and Jerry hadn't heard from him."

Paine asked her to give him some telephone numbers, and she was busy for a few minutes digging them out of her purse and writing them down. Paine sat back and let hot air move over him. He thought fleetingly of the lake upstate; the bass would be starting to jump in another hour and, from the blue look of the skies, it would have been a clear if hot night for the telescope—he had wanted to look at the Veil nebula in the constellation Cygnus, and there was a double star, two stars orbiting each other that appeared a beautiful contrast of orange and green in the eyepiece, which he wanted to find in Boötes. . . .

Terry slid the paper with the phone numbers across to

him. She seemed about to say something, then turned instead to straightening the contents of her purse. Paine waited for her.

She finished with the purse and looked up at him. "I have to talk to you about payment," she said.

Paine almost laughed. "Terry . . ."

"I won't make a discussion out of it. I'll pay your usual rates."

"We can talk about that later."

"We'll talk about it now, Jack. I insist. I called you because you're a friend, and because you know Bobby so well, but also because you're good. Bobby always said that . . ."

There was something else, something she didn't want to get to, something that looked to make her more embarrassed and less in control than anything they had talked about.

"Terry, what is it."

Her eyes flared in anger. And yet, through her building rage, she remained mute.

"Terry—"

"Dammit, Jack, he took the money! All of it! He emptied the savings account, the checking account, he cashed the CDs and savings bonds." Her fury crested and she brought her fist down impotently on the edge of Paine's desk. She stifled a sob. She looked up at him, her pleading look returning. *"He emptied the girls' college funds, for God's sake! Oh, Jesus, he's gone. . . ."*

Her sobbing went on, and she suddenly looked very small sitting in the chair across from Paine.

He rose and went around to her, and held her and she put her head against him. "I'll get a job, I'll borrow, but I can't pay you now, Jack. I can't. . . . "

He told her to be quiet, that there was nothing more to say as far as payment was concerned, and he held her and let her cry, and suddenly he wasn't thinking of the heat or of jumping bass or stars, but of finding someone he very badly wanted to talk to.

▽

3

THE AIR CONDITIONER IN Jim Coleman's office was off. Coleman didn't look happy about it. It looked as though he had tried to wedge a crack open in the window above the air conditioner fitting and failed; the screwdriver he had used was still stuck at an angle between metal and wood.

Coleman's tie was loosened, his white shirt unbuttoned and the sleeves rolled up. Sweat marks showed through the white polyester around his armpits. His thin face bore a sheen of sweat from his receding hairline down over his dachshund's face to his chin.

"Fucking city," he said, motioning Paine to sit down. "Ever since that housing business last year made the national news, we all gotta be saints. Now we can only have the fucking air conditioning on from twelve to three. Yonkers never had any money anyway, I don't know what they're worried about. You really think Paducah gives a shit about Yonkers?"

"I wouldn't know," Paine said.

Coleman waved at the air. Paine watched a drop of sweat fall from his chin to his clean blotter. "Fucking city."

Coleman looked at Paine for the first time. "So how you been, Jack?" His voice almost sounded as if he cared.

Paine shrugged.

"Ah, I know," Coleman said. "I know." He waved at the air again, stopped looking at Paine. "We really squeezed you through the ass-pipe."

Paine said nothing.

Coleman gave a hearty false laugh. "I always said you looked like shit anyway, right?" The laugh trailed away.

Paine still said nothing.

Coleman wheeled abruptly in his swivel chair, smacked the On button on the air conditioner. "Fuck it," he said, swiveling back around. Again, he looked at Paine. "For you, for old times, I'll break the rules."

The air conditioner clacked, began to throw tepid air into the room.

"Can't we just talk about Bobby?" Paine asked.

"Sure," Coleman said. "Sure. But first we gotta talk about you and me."

Again, Paine was silent.

"Look," Coleman said, "if it helps, I'm sorry. Real sorry. We fucked up twice. I knew your dad, I knew you, but I also knew Joe Dannon. Dannon had a lot of pull around here. I didn't know he was a bad cop. Not that bad, anyway. That whole bunch of us came up here from the Bronx, we were tight. Jeez, you know I served with Petty in Vietnam. Your dad was the guy we all looked up to. You remember me over at the house when you were a kid. You remember we played ball, you and me and your brother Tommy. Your dad bled blue, Jack. But you gotta remember, me and Dannon were partners for six years. From '63 to '69. I was with him on Fordham Road, day Kennedy got shot. We covered a lot of shit together. We got called down to Columbia for the riots. Dannon took stuff, then, small stuff. Just about everybody did. Before Knapp and all that."

"Did you?"

Coleman blinked, then looked defiantly at Paine. "Yeah, I did."

He leaned forward now, over his desk toward Paine, and little drops of sweat fell from his chin to his clean blotter. The air conditioner had not helped the room much.

"But you gotta remember, Jack. It was the times. It was *small* shit. I never saw Dannon do anything more than that. I thought he was *clean,* as far as clean goes. He was my friend."

Coleman leaned back in his chair. "Shit, you should have heard the way he talked about you when you were a rookie in '78 and they assigned you to him. Like you were the worst fucking partner a guy ever had. He had nothing good to say. After a week, he had me believing it, everybody believing it. Except Petty, of course."

"Can we talk about Bobby now?" Paine asked.

"Sure!" Coleman shouted. "Sure, we'll talk about Bobby. But you gotta *understand.* There was no reason to doubt Dannon. I had a lot of pull by then, and I helped him. *I* got you reviewed, *I* got you busted down. It was *me.* Nobody made me do it; Dannon pulled my arm but he didn't twist it. I did it because I wanted to. I believed you were holier-than-thou, a little shit. Your old man, God rest him, was a little like that. It was easy to believe you were worse."

Coleman slumped in his chair; cooling air from the machine behind him moved lazily through his thinning hair but didn't reach to his face. "You know," he said quietly, "I can get you back on the force if you want."

Paine's face registered some surprise. "Let's talk about Bob Petty first."

"All right," Coleman said. "If that's what you want. The bottom line is, he called me up and told me to go fuck myself, which is something he's said before to my face, but this time I believed him."

"Why?"

"We both know Petty," Coleman said. "You can tell when he means something. This time, he meant it."

"Did he quit?"

"He did more than that. He said I could take all his citations and shove them up my ass. That I could take his whole record and burn it."

"Was he drunk?"

"He was drunk. But he was serious."

"Any idea where he was calling from?"

"Someplace busy. Pay phone in an open place, sounded

like. Bus terminal, airport, train station. It didn't sound closed in, like a bar."

"Could you tell if there was anyone else with him?"

"He talked fast and didn't stop."

"Did he give you any idea where he was going?"

"No."

Paine checked a notepad he had with him. "What was he working on?"

Coleman looked away from Paine, looked at the ceiling, looked back. "You know I'm not supposed to talk to you about that."

Paine kept his gaze steady.

"You didn't hear this from me," Coleman said. For the first time in their conversation, his look was rock hard, and stayed that way until Paine nodded.

Coleman said, "You remember Hermano?"

"Yes."

"Well, Hermano has been doing turn work for us. He was facing five to ten and didn't feel like getting fucked in the ass anymore. So Petty had him set up in a drug business, showing some new people interested in moving in all the connections in lower Westchester. He was talking to Petty every week. It was slow going."

"You think Bobby leaving has anything to do with this?"

"Like I said, we both know Petty. It would have to be something else."

"Anything happen to him yesterday, a phone call, someone come to see him that could have set him off?"

"Not that I know of. But he's been a lone wolf for a long time. He didn't tell anybody anything."

"Is that your way of saying you were trying to bust him down next?"

Coleman began to turn red. "Now, I didn't say—"

"You don't have to say anything. We both remember what happened when he stuck with me after Dannon went after my ass. We both know what happens to a cop when he tells everybody he works with to fuck off."

"Nobody—"

"I'm sure nobody said anything out loud. I bet after he left the locker room the middle fingers went up, though. Petty is the toughest bastard I ever met, much tougher than you or I will ever be. He could live with it. He knew what you and Dannon were going to do. If Dannon had gotten the case reopened on me, it would have meant his badge. You would have made sure of it this time."

Coleman said nothing, let the air conditioning blow over the back of his head.

"You said something before about giving me my job back?" Paine asked pleasantly.

Coleman looked as though he'd swallowed something very sour. He looked past Paine's head for a long time. His eyes had taken on the rock hardness evidenced earlier; with an effort of will, he reshaped and softened his face before he let it drift back to Paine.

"A lot of what you've said is true," he said. "I admit that. But Joe Dannon's dead. The investigation of what happened between you and him is closed. You've been completely exonerated. I could start you again, at current pay levels, at exactly the same spot you left in. And, due to extenuating circumstances, I could see that your move toward detective's rank was expedited. I think I owe you that much, and more."

"Is your ass on the line, Coleman?" Paine asked, smiling.

"No," Coleman shot back.

"That's not what I heard. I heard a shake-up is on the way, with this new guy as chief. And you figure on strengthening your position by getting me back on the force and making everyone see what a great guy you are, never mind a cracker jack administrator."

Coleman was looking down at his blotter. "I could assign you to find Bob Petty, at full pay, on leave. You'd be doing just what you are now, and get paid steady for it. You know he wiped Terry out. She must have told you that."

"She told me," Paine said, getting up, "but I don't give a fuck about money."

"You should," Coleman said. "Like I said, with full pay—"

"Did Bobby say anything else to you on the phone?"

"No."

Paine was about to get up, but he found himself pinned, Coleman leaning across his desk, his hand gripping Paine's arm. There was a look of desperation in Coleman's eyes that Paine wanted to relish but discovered he could not.

"Look," Coleman said, "come back and work for me now, and I'll push you faster than you thought possible. In six months, you'll have Petty's old job. Full detective, full pay, accrued pension. I can *promise* that. Do it for your dad." Coleman tried to smile; it came onto his face crooked. "Just like old times, eh?"

"There weren't any old times," Paine said. He pulled his arm away from Coleman's grip, got up, and walked to the door.

As he opened it he looked back. Coleman was sinking slowly back into his chair. The breeze from the air conditioner was rustling the back of his head again; again, none of the coolness was reaching his sweating face.

Coleman looked at him, a haunted look, a look that perhaps was searching for the old times he so desperately wanted to cling to. Then his hands moved around his desk, looking for papers to rustle, and his eyes looked down, a new drop of sweat falling from his face to the center of the empty blotter.

"Better turn your air conditioner off," Paine said, leaving the door open behind him. "I might call the mayor and tell him you're cheating."

$\triangledown$

4

PAINE SAT IN HIS CAR. The road he had parked on sported uncollected garbage spilling off the curbs, cracked brick-face buildings, rusting grates over bodega windows, Miller beer signs behind iron-reinforced windows with only the neon on the *M* flashing sporadically. The entire street looked like an alley.

Ah, America, Paine thought.

Paine lifted his watch to check the time; as he did so, there was a tap on the passenger-side window and he looked over to see Roberto Hermano's smiling face. Hermano was almost woman-cute, with tight black curls, limpid brown eyes with long lashes. His skin was smooth and unblemished. He was twenty-six, but looked seventeen. Paine's watch said 5:45; Hermano was precisely on time.

Paine leaned over and unlocked the door, and Hermano slid into the seat, slammed the door behind him, and relocked it.

Hermano flipped the switch on a miniature boom box he had set in his lap; a blurt of reggae music came out, very loud, before Paine hit the Stop button and said, "Don't."

Hermano smiled widely and then feigned hurt. "Paine-man, how you doing? Don't you *like* Bob Marley, man? I *like* Bob Marley." He moved his face closer, lowering his voice conspiratorially. Paine smelled garlic and marijuana, a sickening mix. "Aroun' *this* neighborhood, man, even if you Puerto Rican, you gotta *like* Bob Marley."

He moved back to his side of the seat, punched Paine

playfully on the arm with his left fist. "So, Paine-man, how you been? You know, I always like you. I like the way you didn't ring my *cujones* the way that Dannon did. Dannon liked to ring my *cujones*. I bet he like to suck them, if he can. That fuck-meat, I hope he rot in hell where he is." He smiled, showing beautiful white teeth. "So, how you been?"

"Not bad. I want to know about Bobby."

"Bobby? Bobby, he *great*, man. He the *greatest*. I got nothing but good things to say about Bobby."

"Do you have any idea where he is?"

"*Me?*" He shook his head vigorously. "No, I got no idea. Like I say, Bobby, he's the greatest."

"Did you know he's gone?"

A wary look clicked onto Hermano's face. "You mean fired? Or like you, busted down?"

"No, gone. He took off, left his family, the police force."

A sickly smile had come onto Hermano's face. "Don't say that, man. Don't joke wi' me, you know it's not nice."

"It's true. I thought it might have something to do with this job you're working with him on."

Hermano shook his head even more vigorously. "No, no, no. Can't be. He can't be gone."

"He is."

"Es'cuse me, man," Hermano said. He fumbled for the door latch, got the door open just in time to vomit into the street. The small boom box started to slip down off his lap and Paine reached over, pulling it back onto the seat.

Hermano retched four or five times, stayed hunched over breathing deeply, then slowly straightened. He closed the car door, locked it. He looked ill when he turned back to Paine.

"You not shitting me, are you?"

"He's gone. Told his wife he's not coming back."

"That's bad. That's very bad. You know, Bobby, he was acting a little edgy I saw him yesterday. I got scared, man. Petty never make me scared before. I jus' thought it was trouble with Coleman, trouble at home." A glimmer of hope sparked into his face. "You here to pick up for him?"

Paine shook his head. "Coleman wanted me back on the force, but I said no."

Hermano was shaking his head again, slowly this time. "Very bad. That Coleman, he'll chuck me to the shit pile now. He never liked Bobby at all. He'll never keep Bobby's promise. They'll put me back in the house. That's something I can't do no more of. No more of that shit. I like women, women like me, no more of that shit. . . ."

"From what I heard, it sounded like they need you."

Hermano brightened. "Really?" His hope dimmed. "No. You heard that from Coleman. Coleman is mean. That Coleman was in the marines, they taught him stuff. Him and that Dannon, they had me in the cellar room once, and they beat me up bad. Dannon liked it. I don't know if Coleman liked it, but he did it. He doesn't know what Bobby had. We had almost nothing. These Jamaicans, they not letting me in yet. Bobby knew that. He told Coleman we were in, the thing was set, we'd be ready to go soon. Bobby was covering my ass." He looked up, smiling like a dead man. "Guess he can't cover it no more, right?"

Paine said nothing.

"I can't do no more of that shit," Hermano said. He groped for his boom box, cradled it, opened the door of the car. "Thanks, Paine," he said. "I always like you."

He got out, slammed the door.

When Paine turned to see where Hermano had gone, he had already disappeared.

$\triangledown$

5

BAD DREAMS.

Paine knew the drill. Get into bed, watch the ceiling for a while until blackness recedes, the pupils adjust, and you can see the whirls of nightlight move across the plaster. A tapestry of life, if you want it to be. Sometimes waking dreams were better; the control room was more at your command, the bad thoughts more easily shunted aside. Sometimes the bad thoughts came anyway, and you felt just sorry enough for yourself, just sufficiently depressed, that you let them wash over you like a black tide, finding that the oily water has bobbed you to the surface and you are floating in shadow light, under the moon of your own past.

There were all kinds of bad dreams. In the past, a century ago in Paine's thirty years, he had taken beer and bourbon to watch the dreams develop. Now he took neither, but the habit his mind had formed with the aid of alcohol had not abandoned him with the departure of the poison.

Rebecca.

Tonight, Paine searched for her on his ceiling tapestry. Paine thought about the gun he had once kept in his bedside table. After meeting Rebecca, he had taken the gun out one night and it had felt like a metal bird in his hand. He had looked down at it and then put it to his head and said, "Bang." The bird-gun had said "Click." There had been no bullets in it, at least not that night; it was only much later, when it was too late, that he had understood why his mock self-execution had mirrored Rebecca's real one; how what she was, the thing that she knew and would not tell him until it was too late, had defined his life from that night onward.

She had been him, Paine's own mirror image, and when she finally told him what he must have known (perhaps he had known it in his dreams—but not on waking, in the tapestry, where it might have done him some good) it was from a short ten miles away on a telephone whose line stretched not ten miles but the opposite way, six thousand miles around the world, because when he had reached her it was too late and she was gone.

"I know that you don't have it in you to do what I'm going to do," she had told him. "You might go to the edge, and peer over, but something will always hold you and keep you from falling. Maybe you'll think of me as holding you from now on," and she had been right, and he had known himself for the first time.

But Rebecca *was* gone. He had lost his mirror self. And even now, always, he would believe that if he had reached her, or been more aware of himself, he could have kept his mirror self with him forever. He could have looked into his own eyes, into his own mind, and seen that part of him that *did* want to do it, and reach into the mirror, through the looking glass, like Alice, and fix the part in her that wanted self-destruction, truly wanted it, and make it live. He had loved her, and she had known that. But it hadn't been enough.

The telephone line had stretched away from him, all around the world, and he had been too late to find out what would have been enough, beyond love, to save her.

Because Paine was sometimes a romantic fool, he thought of her often when he was using the telescope. She had told him, on that phone before she let the receiver drop and hung herself, "I want you to remember that, Jack. I love you. If there's anywhere after this, I still will." When he used the big white tube to peer into the darkness of space, to find the delicate tendrils of glowing gas, the sparkling pinpoints of colored light called stars, the soft, infinitely distant whirls of light that were galaxies, he thought of her as between the stars, between the worlds, perhaps looking down at the distant earth, so tiny to her after death, and seeing him. He knew it was foolish to search for her in the black cold between stars, but it was a way for him to know that she was still with him.

Maybe you'll think of me as holding you from now on.

He was foolish and romantic enough, and knew himself well enough now, to do that.

He searched for Rebecca in the ceiling tapestry, in the waking dream that rolled over plaster, as always; but tonight Bob Petty's face appeared to him. And it was not Bobby's face he saw so much as Terry's. He saw them together, and knew that what he saw could not be false. All the years they had been together, the looks of secret life that had passed between them, could not have been manufactured by either. They had fought, and loudly; sometimes they had come to the edge of fissure. But there had been something in their union, some dovetailing, that had always locked them so tightly together, for all the world to see, that what had happened, what seemed to have happened, had to be false. They had worked at their marriage; had realized from the very beginning that love was work, and over the years that Paine had watched them, the work had produced something as tight and true, at the core, as any work of art.

Paine believed in secret lives. He believed it because he knew it to be true. All men keep secrets, especially from themselves, and all unions have secret lives. But the essential self is rarely hidden to those who really look. Most of our lives are spent in self-absorption; our dealings with those others of our species are carried out in the most superficial fashion. The neighbor is always startled on hearing that the "nice, quiet boy" next door has murdered his family; that same neighbor would blush with embarrassment on reflection, to realize that for the fifteen years he'd known the nice, quiet boy, he had had no interaction of consequence with him.

All men have secret sins. Paine believed this implicitly. He could believe in Bobby Petty's infidelity; could believe in any of a number of secret sins: gambling, transsexualism, homosexuality. No revelation, no tiny room exposed when the secret key was turned, would surprise him.

But just as all men have secret lives, so too do they have essential selves, and these they wear like a shroud. No mask can hide it from those who look. Had that neighbor chosen to look to the human being, not the docile mask, of the boy next door, he might have discovered the six-year-old who killed frogs for the pleasure of it, the eight-year-old who torched the curtains in the living room to test the reaction of his distant parents. The essential self leaves clues no man can hide. It transcends the secret self.

Bobby Petty had violated his essential self. Whatever his secret life, he had done something to destroy what he himself was. This was no crime of passion, of secret lust, of suddenly uncontrolled or unbearable passion long hidden. He had deliberately, and coldly, cut the roots from his own soul, and this was what bothered Paine so much.

And Terry knew it, too. It was the source of her unmooring. It was not the fact that her husband had abandoned her—not even the fact that he had taken their money and terribly insulted their children. These were common things in the world, and Terry Petty was a person who could handle such things. What she knew in her gut, and what had frightened her to the core of her own being, was that Bobby had violated not his mask but himself.

And so the tapestry rolled across Paine's ceiling. In his shorts and T-shirt, with his hands locked behind his head, in the hot night with his fan blowing hot air across his sweating face, the fan with the loose part that could never be tightened, which always made a slight ticking noise—with all of this around him, Paine saw the close detail: Petty with his two girls, one on either knee, stealing what he thought to be a private look of undisguised pride, a smile of such warmth, looking at no one but himself, his own mirror; Petty drunk, to the point where some of those little secret

rooms open up, crying, hating himself for crying, telling
Paine about his four-month affair, his disgust at his own
carnal need, his disgust at his own weakness, the marine
training, the Catholic roots of his education, the code of his
police office all coming to tell him how weak and human he
really was, how unworthy, the tears tracking his rock-hard
face, his fist hitting the table and staying there, even as the
upset Bud bottles fell to the floor, his fist trying to grind into
the wood of the table, become part of it; and then his tear-
streaked face had turned to Paine, the tears etching along
the rock hardness, and he had looked at Paine and grimaced,
a grimace that was almost a smile, and shaken his head and
said, "But Jack, I *enjoyed* it! I *wanted* to do it! I've been
married to Terry for fifteen years, I've loved her for twenty, I
love my family and would die for them on this *spot*"—again
he had banged the table, bringing a look from the bartender,
who knew them but knew that cops could be violent, even
dangerous, especially when very drunk at three o'clock in
the morning—"but *Jesus*, Jack, I did it because I wanted to.
What the fuck is wrong with me?"

He'd sat up then, and laughed at his own incompre-
hensibility.

"We all do shit we shouldn't," Paine had said.

Petty's self-anger flared again. "That doesn't answer it!"
He leaned close over the table, as if the empty booth were
surrounded with ears. "You know Terry," he said. "You've
seen her in a bathing suit. Even after having kids her body
drives me crazy. It's not perfect, but it's . . ." He'd shrugged.
"It's perfect. You keep telling me how wonderful she is."

"She is, Bobby."

Petty snorted, sat up straight, searched for a still-usable
bottle of beer, found a tall-neck Bud hiding near his elbow half
full. He drank from it. "She is. And she knows it. That's what
I've always loved best about her: She knows she's good at being
a wife and a mother, she's strong—" Petty waved his own
thoughts away. "All that shit." He looked at Paine. "Didn't you
tell me once you'd grab her in a minute if I was gone?"

Paine smiled. "I was drunk, Bobby."

"You're drunk now. Tell me, wouldn't you grab her in a minute if I wasn't around?"

"Sure I would, Bobby."

"I'm not kidding." Petty was very drunk. He put his beer bottle down, almost tipping its edge, and reached across the small table to grab Paine's arm in a vise grip. "Didn't you have a crush on her when you first met her? She told me you tried to kiss her once at one of the Fourth of July parties down at the club." His eyes were as intense as his grip, which meant that he wanted a straight answer.

"I did, Bobby. But I was drunk then, too. By then I had Ginny."

"Yeah," Petty said. "Sure, Ginny . . ."

The bartender was making motions with his arms to Paine. Jack focused his eyes toward the bar and saw the man waving his apron like a flag. When he caught Paine's attention he pointed to his wrist and waved at the door.

"Pete wants us to leave," Paine said to Bobby.

Bobby turned and smiled at Pete. "Out in a minute, Petey."

Pete threw up his hands and turned to his paper on the bar, flipping the pages angrily. Bobby found his Bud bottle, drained it, then suddenly returned his tight eyes to Paine. "You didn't answer my question, Jack."

"Which one?"

Again, tears forced their way out of Bobby's eyes; the tightness in his pupils softened and his granite face flushed red.

"Don't hit the table," Paine said, quickly putting his hand out to stay Petty's fist.

"Dammit, Jack, I want to know! I want to know why I let my dick tell me what to do! Terry's great in bed, she's the best! I felt so guilty. . . ." His face had collapsed into his hands, and he sobbed like a schoolboy. "Jesus, I couldn't wait a couple of months till she got well. I was too fucking weak. I'll never do anything like that again. . . ."

He sobbed for a half minute; then Paine stood and got him up and steered him for the door, past Pete shaking his head over his paper, stretching to come after them and lock the door, mumbling with a trace of affection, "Fucking cops . . ."

That was Bob Petty. He'd never do it again. He'd been a weak marine. A weak cop. And could barely stand it, the breaking of his code.

That was Bobby Petty, the essential Bobby Petty. There were secret doors, and secret locks into little hidden rooms, no doubt, but that was Bob Petty's soul.

He'd never do it again.

And now he'd done it again, broken the code, kicked the pieces into the gutter, and Paine couldn't figure why. Petty had unlocked some secret door, and whatever was in it was so deep and horrible that it had made him take his essential self, the soul of Bobby Petty, and strangle it and make it die.

Paine stared at the ceiling, at the parade of his waking dreams. This night, even in waking, none of the images came together and made sense. He stared a long time, in the heat, with his hands cradling the back of his head, and still Bobby Petty's soul stayed in front of him, inviolable, rock hard, refusing to break, and so none of the questions were answered.

Sometime late in the hot night, Paine's eyes closed, and the waking dreams stopped, and the subconscious took over with its own jumbled version of life. Paine dreamed sleeping dreams, bad dreams, too, and in them he searched for Rebecca between the stars, wanting desperately for her to reach out to hold him from a place he could not see, as he looked up into the starry void from a place he would not leave, but still did not want to be.

$\triangledown$

6

H E CALLED TERRY EARLY, giving her enough time, and when he got there, the house was straightened and the children were out to school and she wore a face that was presentable to the world. She looked as though she had stopped crying, even when alone. She looked halfway back, which might be as far as she got for a while, but it was enough.

Paine sat at the kitchen table, and she had coffee ready. She wore shorts and a gray gym T-shirt that said Police Academy on it. It was eleven o'clock in the morning, and the temperature was already eighty-five degrees. The weatherman had said high nineties, maybe the century mark.

"I want to look through the house, Terry," he said. She was studying his face, and he was sure she already knew what he meant, and understood, but he said it anyway. "Top to bottom. It'll look like it's been burgled when I'm finished. I want to go through his clothes drawers, the junk drawer he kept stuff in, his toolbox, the glove compartment in the car. I want to go through the last week's trash, his uniforms. If you want to leave while I'm doing it—"

"I'll help you."

"All right," he said. "But I just wanted to tell you it might be painful—"

She shook her head, cutting off his argument against her helping.

Paine drank his coffee, trying to think of something to say to her. She sat holding her untouched coffee mug, letting the steam take the warmth out of it. He knew she was waiting

for him to say something to her, one way or the other, to tilt
her life toward 100 percent.

"I take it no one's heard from him again," he said.

She shook her head no.

"I talked to Coleman yesterday afternoon, and then
Hermano, the guy he was working on the drug bust case
with. Coleman acted like an egg on a griddle. I think they're
coming down on him from up top. He tried to get me to rejoin
the force."

"Christ."

"Coleman always was an asshole. But now I think he real-
izes it for the first time. Hermano was just scared. I don't think
this had anything to do with what Bobby was working on."

Her fingers working on the handle of her coffee mug, she
waited.

"Terry," he said, "I'm as blank as you. I don't have any
idea what this is all about. That's why I want to go through
the house—"

"Then let's do it," she said angrily, getting up.

They started in the basement. Bobby had a workshop
down there, one half of the cellar behind a Sheetrock barrier
that was all his own. There were two workbenches, one
covered messily with tools, fuses, rolls of duct tape, tubes of
glue; the other immaculate, a fisherman's shrine, neat racks
of lures above neatly labeled drawers of miniature tools and
fly-tying equipment.

Paine went through everything, the drawers, the boxes,
the discarded shopping bags with abandoned receipts inside.
When he finished in the toolroom he went through the other
half of the cellar, the playroom, which contained only toys
except, on one side under a low Tiffany-style fluorescent, a
pool table, now piled high with boxes of military novels and
sealed Christmas ornaments. Paine checked down the slip-
covers of the two old chairs in the corners, moved the canned
food shelves under the stairs.

"What's next?" Terry asked.

"Where does he keep the rest of his stuff?"

"Mostly in the bedroom. The garage, too."

"The garage, first."

They went to the garage. Paine checked under the seats in their Plymouth Voyager, slid his fingers up under the dashboard, lifted the ashtrays in the back seat to check the wells. There were open cartons of oil and bags containing power steering fluid, transmission fluid, an oil filter. He found nothing but receipts.

"Okay, Terry, let's look at the bedroom."

The bed was made; there was a quilt with pastel squares framing yellow and blue geese. The chest of drawers was tall, four long drawers and two half drawers at the top; it was mahogany, with Queen Anne legs; on top of it was a silver tray holding perfumes and a black glazed ceramic whale with the back scooped out for a change holder.

Paine went through the change holder; there was change and a couple of receipts from Sears, a pocket comb with a couple of tines missing, a Sears wallet photo of the two girls and Terry, all of them smiling, bunched together, Terry in back with her arms around them. Paine looked at it for a minute, then put it back.

"Which drawers are his, Terry?"

She was standing behind him, arms folded. "Bottom two."

The room was hot. There was a small air conditioner set into one window, but it wasn't turned on. The room was dark, blinds down, thin slices of heated light thrown against the far wall. A dressing mirror slanted downward, reflecting floor and bed at an angle.

Paine pulled open the bottom drawer. Folded Izod shirts, no pockets; shorts, pockets empty. Two pairs of jeans. Behind, on the left side, a cluster of papers, insurance policy sheets, car registration forms, police benefit department information.

"He stored all the important papers there," Terry said behind him.

Paine put the papers back, slid his hand to the right along the back length of the drawer. An unused belt coiled like a snake, a package of unopened handkerchiefs. Two pairs of folded chinos, pockets empty. In the right far corner, a blue rectangular box. Paine pulled it out: a twelve-pack of Trojan condoms, two left.

Behind him, Terry said nothing. Paine put the box back.

The upper drawer was filled with boxer shorts, T-shirts, a folded pair of flannel pajamas that looked unused. White crew socks, black nylon stretch socks. A flat, wooden, hinged box in the right front with more change, another comb, more receipts and paper clips in it. Under it was a bill in a long brown envelope. He lifted it out, studied it: a doctor's charge with an outstanding balance that he realized the import of as Terry spoke.

"That was from the second miscarriage," she said. He turned on his haunches to look at her: her arms folded, seemingly cold in the hot room, hugging herself. "There was some question about insurance payment, so they told us to wait on the bill."

"I'm sorry, Terry," Paine said.

Her reply was too quick. "Don't be."

Paine looked at her a moment, turned away, slipped the bill back into its place and closed the drawer.

He stood, stretched his back. "Let me look at the closet," he said.

There was one closet, long sliding doors. She owned two-thirds of the left side; Bobby's clothes had the rest. Paine slid the door over, went through the two suits, the dress uniform. There were six white shirts, two blue, a couple of sports shirts with twin breast pockets. Another pair of chinos, hanging. There were three pairs of shoes, a pair of Adidas, the floor behind them was clean.

"He took nothing with him," Paine said, standing.

"No."

"Let's look at the laundry," Paine said.

She turned. Paine followed her out into the hallway. She stopped by the bathroom door. "Here." Just inside the bathroom door was a white wicker hamper, stuffed to overflowing.

"I haven't done wash in a few days," she said. She opened the hamper, began to pull clothes out. The top was filled with girl things that she tossed aside; about halfway down were a couple of Bobby's shirts, which she handed to Paine. He went through the pockets, found nothing. There was another shirt at the bottom of the hamper, a long-sleeved sport shirt, wrinkled, that looked like it might have been there for a while. Again, nothing.

"What about the washing machine?"

Without speaking, she walked past him, down the hallway beyond the kitchen, opened a door into the laundry room.

Paine went in, snapped down the door of the dryer. It was empty. He pulled up the door on the washer, found a load of wash filled to the brim, blue liquid laundry detergent drying like a stain over the clothes on top.

"I was doing that when he decided to go out the other night," Terry said. "I never turned the water on."

Paine lifted the top clothes out; two of Bobby's shirts. He got damp blue detergent, mildly sticky, on his hand. He went through the pockets on the first shirt. The second one had a folded piece of paper in the left breast pocket.

A leak of blue detergent had reached into the paper, dying it. Paine unfolded it, held it up toward the light.

In Bobby's hasty scrawl was written: AA Flt. #85.

Paine handed the note to Terry. "Recognize this?"

She looked at it; she didn't recognize it, but she knew what it was. She knew Bobby's handwriting well enough, was smart enough to know what it was, what it meant.

Paine gently took the paper from her; if she had been halfway back before, she was back to zero again. She clasped her hands together, not finding the solace she needed, and then she leaned into Paine, folding against him, her hands opening to clutch him, digging into him as if he was a human life raft. She began to weep again, and he felt her body shaking against him.

"Oh . . . Jack . . . I still thought . . . maybe he was just drunk . . . just on a bender, maybe he . . . was calling from a bar somewhere nearby. . . . I was stupid, but . . . I still hoped. . . ."

Paine put his arm around her and held her, and let her cry.

And with his other hand, he held the paper up and looked at it, and knew now that there was somewhere to go.

7

Paine HAD PICKED UP his phone to dial when Anapolos came into his office. He put the phone down.

"Sit down," Paine said.

"I'll stand, Mr. Paine," Anapolos said. He was a short man who always looked as if he were charging forward. His head was large, nearly bald. The top part of his body was barreled, on top of short legs. He was a Greek from Astoria, Queens, whose brother-in-law had sold him a building in Yonkers, telling him that it was a way to get rich and make his sister happy. Paine knew that the brother-in-law had been right.

"This . . . *letter* I get from you, Mr. Paine," Anapolos said, waving a folded sheet of paper. "I don't like it."

"You weren't supposed to like it," Paine said. "I had a lawyer look at it before I sent it to you. He said I was right on every count, and that, if I wanted, he'd help me bring you to court."

The top of Anapolos's head reddened. He leaned closer to Paine's desk, hammering the paper down on it and raising his hand into a fist. "You are not a good tenant, Mr. Paine."

"You're a shitty landlord, Mr. Anapolos. When I moved in here in February there was no heat. I've seen five different species of roaches. There is at least one family of rats on this floor; I've seen others on outings in the lobby and in the storage area in the basement." Paine pointed to the piece of paper Anapolos had put on his desk. "I listed enough building code violations, especially blocked fire exits, in that paper to have you shut down and fined till it hurts. The lease I

signed with you promised air conditioning, and that micro-
wave oven in the window hasn't worked since GE put it
together in 1963. I don't like the way you run your building,
Mr. Anapolos."

"And I don't like you, Mr. Paine. You're not a nice young
man."

"I'm not so young, Mr. Anapolos."

Anapolos straightened slightly, put his hands on his hips.
Paine was suddenly reminded of pictures he had seen of
Mussolini. He almost laughed.

Anapolos raised one finger, and suddenly Paine did laugh.

"This is not funny, Mr. Paine. I am going to have you
evicted." Anapolos pronounced the last word like a curse.

Paine shook his head; he could not stop laughing.

"You will hear from me again, Mr. Paine!" Anapolos said.
With a flourish he spun on his little shoes and walked to the
door, leaving his paper behind on Paine's desk.

Anapolos opened the door, closed it loudly behind him.

"Jesus Christ," Paine said. He took the paper Anapolos
had left, slipped it into a fresh envelope, addressed it to the
landlord and put it in his Out box.

This time he picked up the phone and punched in a
number.

The 800 number rang twice and he was connected to a
computer voice that asked him to wait until an operator was
free. Phone music played. Paine angled the phone away from
his ear until a voice came on the line; it was the computer
voice, asking him to please be patient. The music came on
again. Paine moved the phone away from his ear until a
human voice said, "American Airlines, may I help you?"

"I hope you can," Paine said. He made himself sound
chagrined. "I'm sorry to bother you about something stupid,
but I think I'm in trouble with my boss. A couple of days
ago I took flight eighty-five out of New York, and I lost my
ticket receipt. I . . . ." he paused, sounding embarrassed,
"well, my boss isn't the kind of guy who believes what you
tell him, and I was wondering if you could get me some sort

of copy of the receipt, a Xerox or anything, just to prove I took the flight. My name is Bob Petty."

The cheery girl's voice said, "I'm certain we can help you, sir. If you'll just wait a moment . . ."

Paine waited; he could hear the soothing tap of computer keys, the pause while the information he wanted was pulled up onto a screen. There was another pause. More muted key tapping.

"That would be Robert Perry?" the soothing voice asked. Paine said yes. She confirmed Perry's address. "That was a one-way ticket to Dallas-Fort Worth?"

Paine said yes again.

"All right, sir. I can have a receipt mailed to you. You are aware that it will be marked duplicate?"

"That's fine," Paine said.

"Is there anything else I can help you with?" the soothing voice said.

"Can you tell me if I connected with another flight?"

There was another pause. Paine didn't hear the immediate tapping of computer keys. He could imagine her trying to put his question into a form that made sense to her.

"Certainly, sir," she said, a little less cheerfully. She probably hadn't succeeded. But he heard the keys tap.

"I show only a one-way to Dallas-Fort Worth, sir. Would you like me to try the other airlines?"

"Please. I have a lousy memory."

A longer pause. No cheerful voice this time. But the keys tapped.

"I show only a one-way on American to Dallas-Fort Worth. Is there anything else I can help you with?"

"Nothing today, thank you."

"Thank you for flying American, sir," she said.

"Sure."

He hung up, then called the 800 number back. He got more recorded messages, more music, and then another cheerful voice came on and he booked a flight to Dallas-Fort Worth.

* * *

As Paine dropped the phone into its cradle it rang. He put it back to his ear.

"Paine?" someone said.

"This is Paine."

"Kevin Bryers. I'd like you to come in and talk, when you have a chance."

"Sure, Chief Bryers. But I won't have a chance for a couple of days."

Bryers paused. "All right. It's about Jim Coleman."

"Not Bobby Petty?"

"That's part of it. Mostly Coleman."

"If it was about Petty I could come now. Too bad."

"You'll come and see me?"

"You going to offer me my old job back, too?"

Bryers didn't laugh. "We'll talk," he said.

"Sure."

Paine hung up the phone, punched another number. It rang a few times, then a sleepy voice came on.

"Wake up, Billy, I'm coming to see you," Paine said.

"Jack?"

"Yes." Paine gave his flight number, time of arrival.

"Great. You coming down to look through my telescope?"

"Not this time, Billy. Business."

"Oh."

"But we can talk."

"Great." Billy yawned. "What was that flight number again?"

Paine gave it to him. "I take it you were out all last night?"

"Yeah."

"Good skies?"

"Real good. Hot as hell, though."

"Go back to sleep, Billy."

"You bet I will. See you later."

Paine hung up the phone. This time when he put the receiver in its cradle, it stayed mute. He fumbled with the message machine for a few minutes until he was reasonably sure it would work, then locked the office and went home to pack.

8

OF ALL THE AIRPORTS Paine hated to fly into, which was all of them, he hated Dallas-Fort Worth the least. There was something about the wide openness of it that inspired confidence. Whenever he came into LaGuardia Airport in New York, he felt as if the pilot were dropping straight down into New York City. If they came in too short they'd be in the water; too long, they'd be on a sidewalk on Fifth Avenue, slamming into the front of Tiffany's. But in Dallas there was prairie to spare; for miles around everything was flat and runwaylike, and, to Paine's mind, the pilot had plenty of room for plenty of errors.

Which wasn't the case, of course; Billy Rader had gleefully informed Paine that Dallas-Forth Worth has a terrible wind shear problem; tornado swirls can rise up out of nowhere, and thunderstorm clouds have a way of rising like tall black walls up to God and slamming rain and hail and wind into everything.

But so far Paine had seen none of this, and today it was high and blue and hot when the plane touched down.

Billy Rader was waiting for him at the gate, smiling through his full beard as he took Paine's bag.

"See the wreck on the way in?" he asked in his pleasant drawl.

"No."

Rader continued to smile. "A 737 buckled its right landing gear yesterday. Slammed into a parked L10-11. Last week we had a near miss between a Delta and Texas Air. Last week an American flight, might have been yours, nearly flipped in the wind." His grin widened. "I know how much you like this airport."

"Did I say that?"

Rader laughed, moving them to a pair of empty gray padded seats in the waiting area. He sat down, stretched his legs. "Okay, Jack, what's up?"

"Remember Bob Petty?"

"Sure. Couldn't get him to look through the telescope, but he was a good fisherman."

"I'm trying to find him. He took a one-way here two days ago. Left his wife and kids and job."

"Jesus. Didn't seem like the type."

"He isn't. Thing is, I don't have any idea why he came to Texas. As far as I know, the only time he's ever been here was that one time with me. He's never mentioned anything about the state, except you and those fucking catfish."

Rader smiled, slapped Paine on the shoulder. "We can't all be good at everything, Jack. If I remember correctly, you did have a nibble."

Paine said nothing.

"Well," said Rader, laughing, "if we get some work done, maybe we can get some viewing in tonight."

"Fine," Paine said. "You still got all those friends in this town you're always talking about?"

"Follow me," Rader said, handing Paine his bag and stretching to get up.

Paine waited on a red plastic seat while Billy Rader talked at the Avis counter. He was there a long time. Whenever Paine looked at him, Rader seemed to be laughing, and the young woman he was talking to laughed back. Finally, the young woman left the counter and Rader followed her into an office. The door closed.

A half hour passed. When the door opened, Billy went back to the counter with the young woman. He leaned on it casually, laughed, and the young woman laughed.

Finally, Billy left the counter and came to where Paine was sitting.

"He didn't rent from Avis," Rader said.

Paine was about to say something when Billy held his hand up. "But he did from Budget. I had to wait for her to access the big computer in the back, with all the insurance stuff in it. The big companies share it. He rented a blue Chevy Cavalier and is staying at a Best Western in Fort Worth. We can get there in a half hour."

Paine smiled in admiration.

"I told you we'd get to use the scope tonight," Rader said.

It was nearly 100 degrees outside the terminal. Paine looked at his watch. Six o'clock. Which meant it was five in Dallas. And 100 degrees.

"Humid, too," Rader said. "Been dripping like a pig for days. I told you it was hot last night. Seventy-five at three in the morning."

"It wasn't even this bad in Yonkers."

"Welcome to Texas!" Rader laughed.

They got into Billy's Ford Galaxy; air conditioning shot out at Paine as Rader gunned the engine.

"Jesus!" Paine said, relishing the cool.

"Feels good, doesn't it?" Billy said. "Let's hope the air conditioner in your friend's room is on."

They reached the motel in almost exactly half an hour, still arguing about what to listen to on the radio. Laughing, Rader won out, threatening to kick Paine out into the hot air unless Dwight Yokum stayed.

"Back in a minute," Rader smiled. He left the keys in the ignition so the radio would stay on.

Paine turned the knob off as soon as Rader was gone.

Billy was back almost immediately. Bending to get into the car, he smiled, reaching over to snap the radio back on.

"Room 414," he said.

They parked in front of the right stack of rooms, looked

for the rented blue Cavalier, which wasn't there. When they had trudged the stairs to the fourth level, stopped before room 414 and knocked to no answer, Paine said, "He's not here."

"He didn't check out of the motel," Rader said, producing a room key from his pocket, slipping it smoothly into the lock and snapping it open, "so who cares if he's here or not?"

"Is there anybody in Texas you don't know?" Paine asked, as they entered the room.

"Just the border guards," Rader answered, laughing, "because I've never left."

Paine snapped on the light.

The room looked recently lived-in. The sheets on one side of the double bed were rumpled; a pair of chinos were draped over the back of the desk chair. A new-looking gym bag was open next to the desk; inside were white socks, boxer shorts, a couple of open-necked shirts, one of them still in its plastic wrapping. The waste basket next to the desk had other opened wrappings in it: a toothbrush box, six-pack of white crew socks, underarm deodorant. The writing pad on the desk was unused.

Paine was checking the night table next to the bed when Rader called to him from the bathroom doorway.

"Don't think you're gonna like this, buddy."

Paine joined him.

Inside the bathroom was a lot of blood. It brightened the white tile around the tub like fresh paint; one smeared section at the back wall resembled a modernist painting, bold downward finger strokes ending in a nearly perfect bloody handprint. The hand that had made it was nearby, cocked away from the wall at a frozen angle. The rest of the body was attached to it except for the head, which was missing.

Rader flipped up the bloody toilet seat with the toe of his boot; inside, staring up at them dolefully from a pool of bloody water, was the missing head.

"Jesus Christ," Billy Rader said.

Paine said, "It's not Bobby Petty."

▽

9

A COP NAMED LANDERS talked with Billy Rader while Paine sat outside the office. Paine heard them laughing. After a while Rader came out, squeezed Paine on the shoulder, kept on walking toward the female dispatcher who had smiled and motioned to him from across the room.

"Come on in, Paine," Landers said, and Paine stood and entered the office.

Landers waited for him at the door, and closed it behind him. He walked around to his side of the desk, and they both sat down. Landers was short and thin, with a pinched, leathery face. He wore a light tan cotton suit with an open-necked shirt.

It was hot in the office. The window was halfway open, letting hot air in, and a rotating fan in one corner next to a row of old oak filing cabinets blew the hot air around.

"Well," Landers said, scratching his cheek before looking at Paine, "if you hadn't been with Billy Rader, you'd be in deep shit. Way I see it, you're still in shallow shit. But that's okay, as long as you do what I say."

"Billy's all right," Paine said.

"Billy?" Landers looked as though his train of thought had been interrupted. "Billy's the best fucking reporter in Texas. He's the only reporter I've ever known who spent time on the force, and the only one who knows what kind of crap we have to put up with. He's always been fair. You're lucky he's a buddy of yours."

"I am," Paine said.

"But you're still in shallow shit. You're from New York,

and I don't like New York detectives down here, especially when they don't check in with me."

"I'm not from New York City. I'm from Yonkers."

Again, Landers's train of thought had been derailed. "That don't make a shit of difference to me. New York is New York."

"We like to think there's a difference."

Landers held up his hand. "Enough chitchat," he said. "Here's the deal, and the only deal. I want you out of Fort Worth tonight. And out of Fort Worth means out of the state of Texas. Billy told me what you're up to. If your friend shows up I'll call you. Right now your friend is in the deepest shit there is. He rented a hotel room, then left it with a headless body in it. I don't know about New York, or Yonkers, but we don't like that kind of business in Texas. But you're not going to do anything about it. I am."

Paine sat silent.

"Is this getting through to you?" Landers asked.

"Sure."

"I'm not kidding, Paine. I find your ass in Texas tomorrow morning, and I'll haul you in on suspicion of murder. I can do it, and I'd enjoy it."

Paine stood, drew out one of his cards and dropped it on the desk. "You'll let me know if Bobby Petty shows up?"

Landers reached over, took the card, put it down in front of him. "As long as you're back at this New York number, I will." He stood, held out his hand. "Nothing personal, Paine. Especially as you're a friend of Billy's. We just do things our own way here."

"Everybody does," Paine said, not taking the hand, leaving the office.

Paine extricated Billy Rader from the laughing dispatcher and a group of three uniformed cops he had gathered. They went out into the dusk. The sun was lowering, but the heat wasn't. They stood for a minute, feeling the heat, watching the clear, cloudless sky turning purple toward blue-black.

"He tell you to go home tonight?" Rader said.

"Yes."

"He meant it. Landers can be mean as a rattlesnake."

"He's a cop," Paine said.

Rader laughed. "Ain't we all. You, me, Bobby Petty, Landers. Just a bunch of fucking cops." He studied the sky, seemed intent on one purpling section about thirty-five degrees up from the horizon. He squinted, then grunted with satisfaction. "North star looks good tonight. Not twinkling. Be a good night for seeing." He cocked his head toward Paine. "Landers said you had to be gone by tonight?"

Paine nodded.

Rader smiled broadly. "Nights go from dusk to dawn in Texas this time of year," he said.

"Okay, Billy," Paine said.

By true nightfall, they had reached Billy Rader's observatory, forty miles north of Arlington. There was a glow to the south, from the big twin cities area, but it was blocked by low hills and cottonwood trees and the sky overhead was black and clear.

Before they entered, Paine helped Billy pull the tin slit back away from the dome. It was big inside, bigger than Paine's own observatory, and the telescope was bigger, a huge cannonlike white Newtonian with a sixteen-inch mirror cradled at the bottom end.

"Gonna try something," Billy said, studying his watch in the near dark, snapping on the red map light near the top of the step ladder used to view through the top end, where the eyepieces went. "Shit, we almost missed it."

Paine helped him move the dome around on its ball bearings. It squeaked and rumbled as the slit circled the sky from east to south. Rader quickly set the stepladder in place, climbed to the top, dropped a powerful eyepiece into place and put his eye against it.

"Thought I could eyeball it, but I'd better set the circles," he said, scrambling down the ladder and consulting the two large setting circles on the telescope's mount, etched with degree marks, by which the scope could find any point in the sky.

"Got it now for sure," Rader said, giving a small grunt of pleasure as he refocused the eyepiece. "Come on up here, Jack."

Billy stood aside, as Paine crowded next to him to look into the eyepiece. He adjusted the focus slightly.

"Jesus."

An explosion of light came into sharp view. A huge, frightening, awesomely packed globe of millions upon millions of pinpoint stars, densely packed to the point of white heat at the center, flowing outward in all directions until tiny, individual stars, each a miniature sun, focused like gems against the black sky.

"Omega Centauri," Billy Rader said. "The biggest fucking globular cluster in the sky. You can't see that sucker in New York, Jack. I can only see it here way low through a couple of trees a little while every night."

As Rader was saying this, the spectacular sight began to fade behind the low hills.

"Let me have a last look," Rader begged, pulling Paine away from the eyepiece.

"You deserve it," Paine said.

Sometime toward dawn, as the distinctive cross of the constellation Cygus, the Swan, sank toward the western horizon, Billy Rader lit a cigarette and asked Paine, "So tell me how you've been."

"I can always tell when you get serious because you light a cigarette," Paine said.

In the red light of the map light, Rader shrugged. "Heard some bad things about you a little back. Sounded like it was tough."

"It was," Paine said.

"She really got to you that bad?" Billy Rader asked.

Paine hesitated, pulling away from the eyepiece, in which

the stately Andromeda galaxy, now overhead, floated like a majestic whirlpool of soft light. "Yes, she did," he said quietly.

Rader nodded, pulled at his cigarette. "It was like that with Janet and me for a while, before we busted up. It's bad enough when they get a hook into your crotch, but when they land it in your gut it's much worse. Like they take a piece of your soul away and keep it."

"It was never like that with Ginny and me."

Rader waved his cigarette, making a line of light with the glowing end. "Just because you marry a woman doesn't mean she has the hook in your gut. Sometimes she gets it in there later, sometimes not at all. Most men, I don't think they know what the fuck they're doing when they get married. It's like they go blind for a little while. Then they wake up. Sometimes they're lucky, and when they wake up the hook is in deep and they can be happy. The rest of us . . ." He shrugged. "Why do you think the divorce rate is so high, Jack? It's because the hook was somewhere, in the groin, in the pocketbook, but it wasn't in the gut. That only happens rarely, Jack. Sometimes the hook falls out later, like it did with Janet and me. I can't fucking explain it."

"Neither can I."

Billy was hesitant again. "It's just that I heard you and this woman . . ."

"Rebecca."

"Well, I heard you almost killed yourself after she did."

"I thought about it, Billy. But that wasn't the first time. I don't think I'll be thinking about it much again."

That seemed to be what Billy Rader had been digging for, and Paine was happy he had found it. Rader threw down his cigarette, and Paine watched the glow snuff out under Rader's boot.

"I imagine that don't make getting over her any easier."

"In a way, it does."

"Oh," Billy Rader said. Then he said, "Let's have one more look at the Ring nebula in Lyra, then we'd better close this sucker up and get you to the airport. Landers means what he says. But that don't mean," Rader continued, "that a good ole Texan like me can't keep looking around a little for what you need to know."

"Thanks, Billy," Paine said as dawn began to rise. "I was just about to ask."

Later, as the plane climbed up in the new hot day that would get hotter, as Paine laid his head back and watched Texas fall beneath him from the window, he thought of the Ring nebula. A gently glowing circle of yellow-orange gas, it very much resembled a ring in the darkness. A ring meant many things. Sometimes it meant emptiness. He had worn a ring on his left hand once, and he had taken it off and the space in the middle of it had been his marriage to Ginny. He had never given Rebecca a ring.

Terry Petty wore a ring, a thin round sliver of yellow-orange gold that encircled her finger. He knew she had a hook in her gut; the ring, therefore, was not just a circle of metal but a symbol of an inviolable, mysterious process. Her finger made the ring whole; there was no emptiness in its center.

Bobby Petty had been a lucky man with, it had seemed, a very large hook in his gut. Paine thought of the headless man in the motel toilet, the look of astonishment in the eyes. Many things could cause astonishment, including the betrayal of a friend, and the stark, sudden viciousness of a cold enemy.

Paine wondered if Petty still wore his ring, or if it had been taken from his finger, becoming only a hole in space signifying, as hard as it was to believe, the destruction of the essential self, the dropping of the hook, and, finally, mere and utter emptiness.

▽

10

PAINE SAW THE TWO men standing awkwardly near the entrance to his building when he went in, so he wasn't surprised when they came into his office. They still looked awkward coming in. One of them glanced behind him nervously, so Paine reached beneath his desk and turned on a switch that activated his hidden tape recorder.

"Can I help you?" Paine asked.

One of them, who was thin and tall with curly light hair and a mustache, closed the door to Paine's office and stood with his hands folded in front of him. The thin one looked at the other one, who was stocky and slightly muscled, with dark hair and eyes, and the stocky one shuffled to Paine's desk and tried to look mean. He looked more nervous.

"We're here to talk to you," he said, gruffly.

"So talk," Paine said.

The gruff one looked at the thin one with the mustache, who shuffled his feet and looked down. The stocky one put the flats of his hands on Paine's desk and leaned on it.

"Someone sent us."

"Who?"

"Jeez, it's hot in here," the one by the door suddenly said. He looked at Paine a moment and then looked back down at the floor.

"We want you to vacate the building," the gruff one said.

"Excuse me?" Paine said.

"Move out," the one by the door added quickly.

The gruff one began to move around the desk toward

Paine, and now the one by the door came briskly away from
it and approached Paine from the other side. The two of them
had finally made up their minds. The stocky one reached
into his pocket, removed a short length of brass tube, and
wrapped his fingers around it into a fist. The skinny one
with the mustache had his wide eyes riveted on Paine now,
his hands balling into fists.

The skinny one reached for Paine first, and Paine stood
and came up at him under the chin. The man made a surprised sound and then Paine turned his attention to the one
with the pipe under his knuckles. As expected, he tried to
use that fist first and Paine easily ducked way from it,
crouching and throwing a solid blow into the man's crotch.
He groaned and sat down heavily on the floor. His hand
opened, the pipe rolling away, and he clutched at his privates.

The skinny one decided to try again. Paine was on him
quickly, kicking him hard in the knee as he rose, and the
man grabbed at his knee and yelled and Paine hit him again.
Paine kicked him sharply in the right side as he lay out flat
on the floor and that seemed to be it for him.

The stocky one had not quite given up; he was on all fours,
trying to rise, so Paine kicked him twice in quick succession
in the rib cage and that was the end of it.

Paine stood over them and said, "You guys wanted to talk
to me?"

"Jesus," the stocky one groaned; the thin one with the
mustache said, "Shit."

"Let's talk," Paine said. "Tell me who sent you."

The stocky one shook his head dully, so Paine kicked him
again in the ribs.

"Jesus!" he said. "Stop it!"

"Tell me who sent you."

"I can't," the stocky one said. Paine made sure the skinny
one was watching and he kicked the stocky one again, harder,
and the stocky one screamed.

Paine went to the other one and said, "Tell me who
sent you."

"Please, let's just forget it," the skinny one said.

"You saw what I did to your friend?"

The man nodded.

Paine kicked him smartly in the side.

"Anapolos sent us!" the skinny one said.

"Who are you?" Paine asked.

The skinny one was moaning, lying on his back, holding his side. "Jesus!"

"You're not Jesus," Paine said. He cocked his foot back and the skinny one stopped moaning long enough to say, "Koval. My name's Koval."

"Who's he?" Paine asked, pointing to the stocky one.

"Kohl," Koval said. "His name's Richie Kohl."

"What do you have to do with Anapolos?"

Richie Kohl had rolled up into a sitting position, arms around his knees. He looked grouchy and hurt. "We live in his building in Easton."

"Pennsylvania?" Paine said. "Anapolos owns a building in Easton, Pennsylvania?"

Koval, the skinny one, nodded. "Two buildings. They're pigsties."

"And what are you if you live in them?"

"We owe him rent," Kohl said.

"Get up," Paine said.

They both rose, warily.

"Here's the story," Paine said. He reached under his desk, turned off the tape recorder. "I see you around here again, I bust your heads. Then I get you arrested. I want you to tell Anapolos he's a scumbag. Got that?"

They nodded, looking like schoolboys caught stealing milk money.

"And if it helps," Paine said, as they slouched toward the door, "You don't owe Anapolos rent anymore. In fact, you've got the next six months rent free."

Koval and Kohl looked at Paine blankly.

"Get out," Paine said.

* * *

Paine closed the door behind them, and turned on his message machine.

Chief Bryers's voice was on the tape immediately. It said, "Paine, call me." The rest of the tape was empty.

Paine punched the number in, and was put through immediately.

"Paine," Bryers said, "I'd like to see you now."

"Still hot with that job offer, Chief?"

Bryers waited a beat before answering. "A man named Roberto Hermano, who Bob Petty was working with, was found murdered. And Coleman has disappeared. I'd like to see you. Now, if you can, Paine."

"I can," Paine said.

$\triangledown$

11

Paine didn't know Bryers well. He had been brought in to clean up the department only six months before and by all indications had done a good job. People were scared of him, which meant he was effective. And he had been Coleman's main worry, which was fine with Paine.

Bryers's office was spartan and neat; the clock on the wall outside said 3:05 and the air conditioner had been turned off. There was a residual breath of cool air that Paine relished as he sat down.

"I hear that you spoke with Roberto Hermano," Bryers said, directly. He looked like the kind of man who didn't waste time. He looked like his office. His tie was still knotted, his shirt white and unstained with perspiration, the sleeves buttoned at the cuff. His face was a bureaucrat's: oval, symmetrical, bland but potentially hard, the eyes unblinking, the hair thinning, parted, always combed. He'd look at home here or behind a lawyer's desk, or a vice president's desk at any corporation anywhere. He looked like the kind of man who would be good at implementing policy, or carrying out orders to the letter. Paine wasn't sure if he liked him or not.

"I talked with Hermano two days ago." Paine smiled slightly; it went unreturned. "Just a friendly talk."

"Coleman told you about him?"

"Well . . ."

"Coleman told you about him," Bryers stated, as if he were reading from prepared notes. "He also told you about Petty's drug investigation. Also, he made an unauthorized job offer to you, with incentives attached that made the offer, in effect, a bribe."

"Can I guess?" Paine said. "You had Coleman's office bugged."

Bryers almost blinked. "I'd like to know what Roberto Hermano told you during your conversation."

"He told me Bob Petty was a good guy, and that now he thought he was fucked because Petty was gone, and the whole operation would be folded. I guess he was right."

Bryers nodded. "We found him in his apartment with his throat cut. His testicles had been stuffed into his mouth."

Bryers waited for a reaction that Paine didn't give, then leaned slightly forward. "The thing is, Paine, I don't want you involved in this."

"Why not?"

"Because you're just going to get in my way. I was sent here to do a job. I've been here six months, and in another few months this police department will be clean."

"Bob Petty isn't a dirty cop."

"I wish I could believe that, Paine. But now I don't think so. We believe Coleman had Roberto Hermano killed. Coleman had been dealing with Hermano ever since Petty's drug sting was set up. When the sting was sprung we were going to bring Coleman down with the rest of them. Now it looks like Petty, too, was on the other side of the fence. I realize Petty is your friend, Paine, and I'm sorry, but that's the way it is."

"I can't believe that."

Bryers leaned a fraction of an inch closer. "We did have Coleman's office bugged, Paine. And his phone tapped. Very legal, I've got the court orders.

"Petty made a call to Coleman two days ago, resigning from the force. He was very abusive and abrupt. There were a lot of expletives. It sounded like he was drunk, but I've listened to the tape and I can tell you there was no doubt he meant what he said.

"That was bad enough, walking out in the middle of an investigation and resigning the way he did. But he made another phone call to Coleman, yesterday. After the call, Coleman left his office and disappeared. The desk sergeant saw him leave, and said Coleman was white as a sheet.

"We went over the tape, and we're sure it was Bob Petty's voice."

Bryers leaned back in his chair, pulled open a drawer in his desk, and pulled out a slim cassette recorder. He put it on the desk between himself and Paine.

"Like I said, I'm sorry he's your friend."

Bryers pushed the Play button. The tape hissed and then a voice said, in a professionally hurried tone, "Coleman."

There was silence. Then Coleman began to say hello into the phone to see if anyone was there and was cut off.

It was Bobby Petty's voice. He wasn't drunk this time. "We're murderers, Joe," he said, as if presenting a death sentence.

Coleman began to say, "Bobby—" but Petty cut him off again.

"Tiny," Petty said, and then one end of the phone was cut off. But they heard air run out of a set of lungs on the other end, and then Coleman's voice, just before the phone was hung up, said, as frightened as a human voice gets, "Oh, God, Jesus."

12

THIS TIME, TERRY LOOKED almost back to normal. There was a firmness around her mouth, a hard set that had never been there before, but otherwise she looked like nothing had happened.

"Hello, Jack," she said, as if Paine had come for a barbecue, or to help stain the redwood furniture with Bobby out back. He might almost have thought that Bobby would come out of the kitchen any moment, if not for the fact that much of Bobby's possessions, the same things Paine had meticulously gone through the day before, were heaped in the front hallway, some of them in open boxes filled to the top.

"What's all this?" Paine asked.

"Trash day is tomorrow," Terry answered matter-of-factly. "There's more of it out by the garage."

Paine noticed just how tight the set of her mouth was when she spoke.

Paine wandered down the hallway to the back bedroom. The two bottom drawers on the chest were out on the bed, empty; the third of the closet where Bobby's shirts and shoes had been stored was cleared.

"Terry, what are you doing?"

She stood in the doorway with her arms folded. "Getting rid of it."

"Why?"

"Because he's not coming back."

"Terry—"

"He called me again, this morning, after the girls left for

school He wasn't drunk this time. He was very cool, not abusive at all. And he told me the same things." She looked Jack straight in the eye, unblinking. "Now I believe him."

"Terry—"

"Maybe you can come over next week and help with the garage and cellar. Take any of it you want. Take all the fishing equipment." Her matter-of-factness had begun to blend into anger. "Just get it out of here."

Once again Paine tried to speak, but her anger carried her through his words.

"You know what that *bastard* told me? He told me to give it all to you. It was like he was talking at his own funeral. 'Give it all to Jack,' he said. 'He likes to fish.' Like he was sitting across the breakfast table from me, talking about divorce."

"What else did he say?"

The matter-of-factness was gone now. "He was *calm*, for Christ's sake! He *knew* what he was saying. No one was making him talk, there wasn't any alcohol in him. When I asked him what it was, what was making him do it, a woman or what, he *laughed*. You know what else he said?"

Paine looked at her face, the fury in her eyes.

"He said I should hook up with you. He said you always liked the way my butt looked in a bathing suit, so I might as well let you see it without the suit."

"Terry, why don't you calm down."

Paine was almost frightened by her anger, her hardness. "I'm fine, Jack. Because now I know what my world is again. Before he called this morning I didn't, but now I do. I don't want you to bother looking for him anymore. I'll pay what I owe you when I can."

"Terry, I'm not going to drop this."

"*Yes, you will!*" she shouted. Paine thought she was going to hit him. "You will because I tell you to! I don't give a *damn* about the reason, that's not why I wanted you to find him. I wanted you to find him because I thought he needed me, that he was in trouble. But he's not in trouble, Jack. The bastard is not in trouble. He's gone."

"Terry, I won't drop it."

"*Get out!*" This time she did hit him, a balled-fist strike on his chest. "I don't want you involved in this! I don't want anybody involved! I'll take care of my family, I'll do whatever I have to!" She propelled him down the hallway toward the door with blows of her fist. "Get out, get out!"

The door was open, and then she slammed it behind him, and he heard her throwing things behind it, things from the boxes near the door, Bobby Petty's things, his shoes and socks and shirts, the buildup of a life ready for the garbage man.

They came at Paine from the alley next to his building. He heard them shuffle out quickly behind him, but he was too late to turn and they both hit him at once. He felt the hard meaty hit of a fist wrapped around metal over his right eye, and the tentative jab of another fist in his side. He almost went down, but they were stupid and waited to see if he would, and he recovered and went at the one with the metal in his fist, driving forward with his head lowered. He pushed the man back into the corner of the building and the air went out of the man with a whoosh.

The other tried to come at him then, but he feinted left and rose to the right and hit the man with an uppercut on the jaw. It was Koval, and Paine watched his eyes go fluttery and roll up into his head as he went down.

There was no one on the street, and Paine dragged Koval into the alley and then returned to pull Kohl in after him. Kohl was starting to breathe again so Paine hit him hard and fast, twice in the groin, and Kohl doubled in on himself and the air went out of him again. Koval wasn't moving. Paine made sure he was breathing, and then went over to Kohl and bent over and pushed his head back so he was looking into Paine's face.

"Are you really that stupid?" Paine asked.

Kohl said nothing; his breath came in little hurt gasps and his hands were clenching and unclenching, trying to breathe for his lungs. He wanted to roll into a fetal position but Paine held his head back, not letting him.

"Got any more of those little brass pipes?"

Kohl seemed to nod, so Paine went into the man's coat pocket and found two more lengths of fist-width tubing.

"A real Boy Scout, right?" Paine said. "Be prepared."

Kohl tried to roll into a ball again. "We were just trying to do what we were told."

"By Anapolos? Didn't I tell you I'd take care of Anapolos?"

Kohl just looked at him.

"Christ, you guys are dumb. You just lost your six months free rent." Paine got up. He looked at Koval; some of the focus seemed to be coming back into his eyes. "Go back to Easton, and forget about me. If you bother me again, I'll have you arrested. If I don't break open your heads first and let your feeble brains drip out. Understand?"

Paine looked at each of them until they nodded assent.

"Fine," Paine said, leaving the alley.

Up in his office, Paine turned on his answering machine. Billy Rader's voice said, "Call me."

Paine called, and Billy answered the phone.

"What is it, Billy?"

Rader laughed. "I just wanted to tell you the skies are supposed to be crystal clear down here tonight."

"Fuck you, Billy."

Rader laughed again. "I also wanted to tell you I got a name on the fellow we found in Bob Petty's hotel room. Parker Johnson. Local boy. No one saw him go into the hotel room. Hold on, let me get my piece of paper." Rader went away from the phone, came back. "I'm just guessing, but would you say Petty was about six foot or so, maybe one hundred seventy pounds, waist size maybe thirty-four?"

"About that."

"Well, Johnson was five foot eight, a hundred forty pounds, waist size thirty." Rader gave a short chuckle. "The clothes we found in the room were Petty's, so he must have still been around. And the desk clerk described him as the man who checked into the room. He never came back to check out."

"Anything else?"

"Well, it seems some of Johnson's friends say he got very nervous a couple of days ago, and suddenly moved out of his boardinghouse."

Paine paused. "This guy Johnson have any record?"

"Clean. His boarding house buddies say he liked to drink, liked the prostitutes now and then, but otherwise was just an okay type."

"Thanks, Billy."

"Jack, any chance your friend Petty killed this guy?"

"I'd like to think he didn't."

"Sure, Jack. Anything else you'd like?"

"Any chance you could get into the airline reservation computers, find out if Bob Petty left Dallas-Fort Worth?"

"I'm already working on that. Also the buses and trains."

"I can't thank you enough, Billy."

"Any chance you'd like to sneak on back here tonight, go out to the scope with me?"

"I'd love to, Billy, but—"

"Your loss, Jack."

"Can I ask how you got all this?" Paine asked.

Rader laughed again. "Your friend Landers has a few rivals in the Fort Worth Police Department. Let's just say I've got a lot of friends in high and low places. I'll get back to you."

"Thanks again, Billy."

"I'll think of you tonight while I look at Omega Centauri."

"Like I said, fuck you, Billy."

$\triangledown$

13

THE FUNERAL OF ROBERTO HERMANO was not an elaborate affair. All those attending, if they hadn't been scattered throughout the church, might have filled one long pew. The church itself was a model of pre-Vatican II Catholicism—a miniature gothic that must have been, in its polished wood and cleaned stained glass heyday, an inspiration to its congregation. Gloomy, dark, muggily cool, with shadows in the corners, the eye was drawn upward to the vaulted, painted ceiling and its now-faded representations of cherubs floating among the clouds.

Paine's eye was drawn to Hermano's mother, a short, weeping woman in black who had draped herself over the casket parked on its gurney at front and center, and refused to move. The priest waited patiently while two or three family members—cousins or uncles or brothers—tried to persuade her to sit down. But she would have none of it.

"My Roberto!" she wailed. "What have they done to my baby!"

Paine knew what they had done to her baby, and he hoped the police hadn't been stupid enough to tell his mother. He was dead, which was enough.

"Roberto! My Roberto!"

The man Paine was looking for was sitting alone in the far right front. There was a weak pool of light to his left, and he sat shunning it, in the shadows. Paine made his way up the right aisle, past the carved stations of the cross on the wall—representations of Jesus dropping the cross, Jesus

being whipped, Jesus being nailed to the cross—and slid into
the pew, in the deeper shadows to the right of the man.

"I saw you come in here," the man said, in a slight Span-
ish accent. He was slim, impeccably dressed. The open jacket
of his silk suit showed a spotless white silk shirt, pale blue
silk tie knotted tight and small and perfect. His face was
smooth as a baby's, the eyes large and brown, the hair pulled
back into a short tight black ponytail. In his right ear was a
tiny gold earring. "You sure as hell didn't try to hide."

"I've got nothing to hide, Philly," Paine said.

"Bullshit you don't. I could get my balls cut off, stuffed in
my mouth, just like Roberto, just for talking to you."

"You don't seem worried," Paine said.

Philly smiled slightly. "I'm not," he said, "because they'd
do it to you first."

"Who killed Roberto, Philly?"

"Good question," Philly said. "The guys who might have
done it are sitting five pews behind us."

Paine turned slightly to see three conservatively dressed
black men. Their attention was on the antics of Hermano's
mother, which they followed with mild interest.

"Are they the South American boys?"

"Let's just say they work for the South Americans."

"Did they kill Roberto?"

"No."

"Then who did?"

"That's what everybody here wants to know."

"Was it Jim Coleman?"

"Maybe. I heard Coleman disappeared. But any of fifteen
people might have done Roberto. He was very smart, but he
was also very stupid. He played a lot of cards, Paine, tried to
make everybody happy. The South Americans think they've
lost a great friend, because he was helping them set up. But
at the same time, he was working for Bob Petty, who was
setting them up. And at the same time, he was working for
Coleman, who was setting himself up with the South Americans for a little piece of their pie when he made sure that

Petty's sting didn't work." In the near dark, Philly moved his fingers up and down. "And there was Roberto in the middle, jerking all the strings. And he was very good at it, too."

"You also said he was very stupid."

Philly turned to look at him in the dark. His slight smile came back. "He's dead, isn't he?"

"What about you, Philly—you finished with drugs?"

The smile stayed. "Look at this body, Paine—does it look like I put drugs into it? You remember the way I used to look." The smile widened. "I'm a beautiful man, Paine."

"One more thing, Philly. Is there any possibility that Bob Petty was on the take?"

Philly looked surprised. "Petty? No way."

"Are you sure?"

"You know, I was thinking about this. With Petty taking off and all. The kind of man he is, him leaving a job behind. I wouldn't be surprised if he was going to catch Coleman too when this whole thing went down. I just couldn't see him leaving like that."

"You think it might have been something else? A woman?"

Now Philly's smile was wide. "What do I know about women? Are you asking me if I think it was a man?"

"Okay, I'm asking you."

Philly shook his head. "You know, Paine, you know a lot, but there's a lot you don't know. It wasn't a man. Not Bob Petty."

"You sure?"

Philly turned his eyes on him in the shadows again; this time, there was no trace of humor in the eyes or around the mouth. "I'm sure. You know, I didn't have to say word one to you, never have."

"I know that, Philly."

"You helped me once, I appreciate that. But that favor went out a long time ago. You were a cop then, you're not a cop anymore." The humor was still absent. "You know, there was a time I wasn't sure about you. You know, I would be very good to you."

"Sorry, Philly."

The humor crept back into the corners of his eyes; the slight smile came back. "No harm in asking, Paine."

"No," Paine said. "Thanks, Philly."

At front and center, the uncles and cousins had managed to get Mrs. Hermano to sit down. The priest had come down off the altar, and was slowly circling the coffin, sprinkling it with holy water. He went back to the altar, returned with an incense burner; raising it up high with one hand, he began to circle the coffin again, swinging the burner, sending puffs of incense toward the ceiling.

Paine got up to leave. As he reached the back of the church the scent of incense reached his nostrils. He turned to see that almost everything was as it should be. The three agents for the South Americans were still regarding the ceremony with interest. A small cloud of incense had reached up beyond the low lights to mingle with the painted clouds and cherubs on the ceiling. And Philly sat quiet, impeccably dressed, in his far corner in the shadows. Only now he had taken out what appeared to be a silk handkerchief, and was silently wiping at the corners of his eyes with it.

$\triangledown$

14

PAINE SAW TERRY GET out of her car as he entered his building, and he held the elevator until she came in.

"How long have you been waiting?" he asked.

Her eyes didn't look at him. "A couple of hours. I tried you at home after the bus took the girls this morning, and then I left a message on your machine."

"I was at a funeral."

"Oh."

"It was Roberto Hermano, the guy Bobby was working with on that drug case."

Now she looked at him. "Did—"

"I don't know what to think. There were things I wanted to tell you yesterday, but you wouldn't let me."

The elevator stopped, and they walked the hall to Paine's office door. Inside, the phone was ringing. Paine got out his keys, but by the time he got the door open the phone had stopped.

"Come on in," he said to Terry.

There was more mail on the floor, and Paine picked it up and threw it on the desk. It was hot and stuffy in the room. Paine threw his jacket on the couch, sat behind the desk, went quickly through the mail.

"I was going to call you yesterday, right after you left," Terry said. She was standing on the other side of the desk, looking down at him. "Last night I almost did. I had a few drinks and went to bed, but I couldn't sleep. I almost called you at two in the morning."

"You should have," Paine said.

Terry paused, then said, "I'm sorry, Jack."

Paine put on a smile. "For what?"

She didn't smile. "I was serious about what I said yesterday. But I shouldn't have done that to you."

"Did the garbagemen come?"

A flush of anger or embarrassment came and faded. "Yes. And they'll come next week for the rest."

"My point was, don't you think you're being a bit hasty?"

"In getting on with my life? When people die, you put their things away and go on."

"Bobby's not dead."

Now her eyes were focused straight on him. "To me he is."

Paine looked at her, and she sat down and put her hands in her lap. "I'm sorry, Jack, but that's the way it is. He's gone now. I know he's not coming back. I have a life to get on with."

"Terry, I'm going to find him, whether you want me to or not."

She stood, still clutching her hands, and turned away from the desk. "I know you will. But I don't want to know anything about it."

He saw her beginning to sob, and he rose and walked around the desk.

She turned, crying, and fell into his arms. Her hands moved up to her face, trying to stop the tears, but then she let them come and put her arms around Paine and held him close to her.

"Oh, Jack, I don't know what the hell to do. . . ."

He held her tight, and suddenly she stopped crying and he looked down and her face was there, and she was looking at him with a hard straight look. She looked almost fierce. Tears had flushed her face, and she reached up and held Paine's neck and pulled his mouth down to hers.

Paine tried to stop her, but she held his neck and suddenly Paine found himself opening his mouth and responding. Her kiss was hard and long. Paine tried to fight her, tried to fight himself, but he melted to her, feeling a cloud move down around him, pushing the world out. He held her a long time and her second kiss was not tentative and hard and fierce but warm and soft. Her kiss lessened and she pulled her mouth away from him and when he opened his eyes she was staring at him hard again, in surprise.

"My God, Jack," she said, pushing him away, and Paine stood there as she ran from the office, leaving the door open, and he heard her running down the hallway and then the elevator came and she was gone.

Paine stood still in the center of his office, and felt the cloud that had enveloped him move away and the heat of the office moved in on him again. He felt changed. But the heat was there, and then the phone rang, and he picked it up.

"Paine," he said.

Someone was on the phone, but he heard no voice. He was about to hang the phone up when the voice came back. "Jack, it's Jim Coleman."

It was Jim Coleman, but it didn't sound like him. The bravado, the nervous swagger, the bluster had been replaced by the same purely frightened voice Paine had heard on the tape in Bryers's office.

Paine said, "Do you know where Bob Petty is?"

"Listen to me," Coleman said. "Please. I want you to meet me. I'll tell you about Petty if you meet me."

"Where are you?"

The silence came back. "I . . ." Again silence. The sound of pure fear. "You know the place. The club. You remember the barbecues. I may already have been followed, I don't know. If I leave . . ." Again the silence.

"What does 'tiny' mean, Coleman?" Paine said. "Who or what is it?"

"Jesus," Coleman said. "Please, Jack. Just come. Now."

Paine heard weeping, and then Coleman hung up the phone.

15

PAINE KNEW THE PLACE. There had been barbecues a long time ago, in another world, when Paine had been a rookie cop and Bob and Terry Petty had first been married, when Coleman had no lines on his face and didn't sweat, and all the other young and old cops had smiled and drunk beer and cooked hot dogs and the smell of hamburgers, which is like no other smell in the summer, filled the big backyard and drifted like smoke over them all, the young and the old cops, and up into the late summer afternoons. Paine remembered it well. He had enjoyed himself here, in the beginning, which was all there was, really, and later, after he was gone from the police, he had heard from Bob Petty that they still had their barbecues at this place but that it wasn't the same. There was no Paine and no Bob and Terry Petty, and Coleman had newer friends then and from what Petty had said they didn't laugh so much, and there was a lot of talk about who was making how much money and where he was getting it. These were the times before Bryers was brought in, and, for a time, there were cops who met at this place who thought they were God, but discovered otherwise.

Paine parked his car not in the empty lot, but around the corner. He had cruised past first, looking for a car that might be Coleman's but there were no cars in the empty lot and the club itself looked deserted, and the picnic tables on the roughly cut lawn sloping down to the railroad embankment, where the trains went by to New York City, were empty and forlorn looking. Beyond the railroad tracks was the Hudson River, and once, at one of those parties in that first and last summer, on the Fourth of July, Paine had sat on one of those picnic tables with Ginny, and watched the fireworks that the river towns sent up, and it had been hot but he had liked the heat, and he had sat with his arm around his wife and, being so young, had thought that this was as good as it got. Later that same night he had gotten very drunk, and tried to kiss Terry Petty.

The clubhouse was a building out in the open near the parking lot, with a bar and locker rooms inside. Paine approached it cautiously. There were no windows open, and Paine used the few trees nearby as cover.

The door was closed, but when Paine tried it, it opened inward into darkness. Paine stepped in and to the side, closing the door behind him.

The bar was deserted, chairs upended onto tables, cords from the bowling machine and the light above the shuffleboard table pulled from their sockets.

Paine moved to the bar and looked behind it. The lights over the mirror behind the bar were off, but he could see that there was no one there.

Paine crossed to the opening of the locker room, and called into the dark opening, "Coleman?"

There was no answer.

Paine moved around the opening into the locker room, snapping on the light switch.

A bank of overhead fluorescents went on, one after another. One rogue lamp began to blink fitfully.

The place smelled of men, and disinfectant, and powdered soap. The floor was tiled white, the walls painted a hearty green that had bleached with time.

"Coleman?"

No sound—not the breath of fear, the cock of the hammer of a .38 Special. Nothing.

Paine moved through the dressing area, past a row of urinals and wall-mounted white sinks. He checked the stalls behind the urinals, pushing the doors slowly back. They were empty.

"Coleman?"

Still no sound, but a coppery smell now, a fresh, hard smell that overwhelmed the disinfectant and powdered soap from the teardrop dispensers on the walls over the sinks.

Paine moved into the shower area.

It was a large room, bleached green walls, gray-enameled cement floors, shower heads at head height in the walls, floor funneling gently to a drain in the center of the room. Something very red had ceased raining into the opening, and was beginning to dry up the slope of the gray floor to the shower wall.

Coleman's torso had been butchered like an ox. The bright smell of blood made Paine gag, but he saw enough of human organs in the split and opened thoracic cavity to fully illustrate a medical textbook. The limbs had been cleanly severed, and lay stacked against the wall. Coleman's head, showing grotesque surprise, had been mounted on one of the shower heads, looking down at the remains of the rest of the body.

Paine's legs grew weak. He turned and walked out, making it almost to the lockers before his stomach emptied. He stood under the flickering neon tube, and there was nothing but the sickening sound of vomitus hitting ceramic until his stomach was dry. It had been that look on Coleman's face, that grotesque look of surprise that said, "Is this how I go?" that did it.

After a while, Paine stood, and pushed himself away from the lockers. He wiped his mouth on his sleeve.

He went back out into the barroom, and went behind the bar. There was a water tap over a deep rectangular aluminum sink, and he turned it on and took a glass from behind the bar and drank. He drank until the taste of vomit and copper receded from his mouth. The water got colder as it ran, and he continued to drink but the taste would not go away.

He left, finally, making his way cautiously back to his car, the taste of death still in his mouth.

$\triangledown$

16

THESE THREE WERE MUCH better than Koval and Kohl. They were waiting in the same alley beside Paine's building, and Paine never had a chance with them. They pulled him deep into the shadows at the back, and after softening him up with belly blows they laid him flat on the ground and one of them held the long cold muzzle of an AK-47 to this temple. A second backed up the first with a .44 Magnum, which he held at arm's length pointed at Paine's mouth.

"You move," the one with the AK-47 said matter-of-factly, "I put six semiautomatic rounds into your mind."

"I won't move," Paine said.

The third one straddled Paine's supine body, standing over him before leaning down to stare into his face. He studied Paine with the same detached interest he and the others had shown at Roberto Hermano's funeral. "I saw you at the church," he said, making it into a slight question.

"I was there."

"Also," the man said quietly, "you were seen talking with Roberto in your car the day before he was killed."

"That's true," Paine said.

The man cocked his head to one side; his face still wore mild interest. "Did you kill Roberto?"

"No."

"Why did you talk to him?"

"I'm looking for someone he knew. A man named Bobby Petty."

The man closed his eyes and nodded. Paine's scalp prickled under the pressure of the AK-47's muzzle.

"One more question," the man said mildly. "Do you know who killed Roberto?"

The muzzle pressed harder into Paine's head.

"No."

The man stared at him, searching, and then he straightened and nodded to the other two men, who pulled their weapons back. Paine felt relief at the withdrawal of pressure on his forehead.

The man folded his hands in front of him and looked down at Paine. "We would like to find the man who killed Roberto. He was our friend."

"Sure."

"If you should find this man, I would appreciate it if you would let us know."

Paine said nothing.

"I'm sorry to have bothered you," the man said.

The three of them turned and walked slowly out of the alley.

Paine lay back a moment, staring at the sky through the faraway slit at the top of the alley. Polite drug dealers with AK-47s was something he did not much want to think about. The AK-47s, he imagined, were what made it possible for them to be polite.

Perhaps if everyone had an AK-47, there would be much more politeness in the world.

It was a thought he entertained for a very short time before he got up.

The first phone message on his machine was from Anapolos, who made several loud threats and then hung up. There was another message after it, from Billy Rader, and Paine called him.

"Good night again last night," Rader yawned into the phone. "Maybe clouds tonight, though."

"What have you got for me, Billy?"

"First of all, your friend Landers is in trouble. Seems he was involved in a minor way with a parking violations thing; some friend of his skimming meters in downtown Fort Worth, and he knew about it but did nothing. It might hurt him, might not. 'Cause of the way he treated you, I called a couple friends of mine still on the *Morning News* and told them where to look for more. Just a hint, mind you, I didn't want to make it too easy. It might snowball, might not."

"Jesus, Billy, I didn't tell you to crucify the bastard."

"Why not? He's been a hard-on for a long time, and anyway, I told you he has enemies. He's not such a bad guy. They used to hang you down here for stuff like that, but not anymore. He'll probably come through intact, but humbled. Humbled is what he needed."

"Is that why you called me?"

"Of course not. I wanted to tell you about my night at the telescope last night."

Paine waited; Rader laughed after a pause.

"Well, okay," Rader said. "Seems Bobby Petty flew back to New York yesterday, American Airlines flight number forty-seven. He used an alias, but one of my friends at the American terminal asked around and found somebody who recognized the description. 'Course it made it a little easier, the alias he used."

"Which was?"

"Bob Paine."

Paine didn't laugh. "Christ."

"Sure, Jack. Want me to see if he left New York again?"

"You can do that?"

"Computers, Jack."

"Sure."

"There's something else, too. That fellow Parker Johnson, I got some background stuff on him. Maybe you'll find it useful. He grew up in Fort Worth, went to school in Fort Worth, was briefly married to a Fort Worth girl from his high school. Two tours of duty in Vietnam, marines, came back and had a hard time of it. Four or five jobs—cook, school janitor, security guard at a mall, early shift at Burger King, that sort of thing. The past year he's been stacking cans in a supermarket. Like I said before, no record, no arrests, no drugs."

"Thanks again, Billy."

"This thing with Landers clears up, you can show your ass down here again. Maybe we can drive out to the desert, visit MacDonald Observatory in west Texas. I know some folks there, get you a look through the big scope."

"Sounds good, Billy."

"Listen, Jack, any idea why Petty would come back to New York?"

Paine told him about Coleman.

"Christ, Jack. That looks bad."

"I'd still like to think he wasn't involved."

"Well, you take care of yourself."

"I will, Billy."

Paine hung up, and immediately made another call.

17

"COME IN, JACK."

The boxes were gone from the front hallway; the garbage-men had come, just as she had said. The house was as clean as ever.

She led him to the kitchen, put a cup of coffee in front of him. She wouldn't look at him, but busied herself at the sink, washing dinner dishes.

The girls were home, watching television in the playroom. Paine heard them alternately laughing and snapping at each other, normal siblings fighting over everything in sight. They came out to see him when he arrived, Mary saying, "Hi, Uncle Jack," shyly and then hiding behind her sister Melissa, who said, "Hi." They looked a lot like their mother, both of them, and Melissa had her mother's straight stare. She looked with it at Paine and it told him she wanted to know where her father was. She looked at her mother at the sink, then turned, and left the room.

"Melissa's having a bit of a hard time," Terry said.

"What did you tell her?"

"I told her her father was gone and wasn't coming back."

"Is that all?"

"It happens all the time," Terry said. "It happened to one of her girlfriends in school last year."

She had turned back to her dishes, refusing to look straight at him.

"I need to talk about Bobby," Paine said.

"Go ahead."

"About his time in the marines."

He could tell that memories were swirling through her, the way she changed the way she was standing, the way she put a wet dish into the drying rack absently.

"What about it?" she said.

"Do you have any records, any pictures?"

"No. He didn't keep anything except his discharge papers."

"Letters?"

A pause. "I threw them out."

"Did he talk about it a lot?"

"No." She let the dish she was washing settle into soapy water, then turned, drying her hands on a dish towel. She looked at Paine now. "He never talked about it, Jack."

"Never?"

"Did he ever talk to *you* about it, Jack?"

"No."

She waited for him to see her point, and he nodded. "I was sixteen when I met him, and he was just going in. He was there four years. In the beginning, his letters used to tell me where he was, what he was doing, his friends, things like that. Then after a while, he stopped talking about it altogether and just talked about coming home. Especially the last two years."

"Didn't you think that was strange?"

"No, Jack, I didn't. I wanted him home. I didn't want to hear about the war. Nobody did,"

"Did he ever mention Jim Coleman in his letters?"

She shook her head.

"Any other names you can remember?"

"A couple of guys in the beginning. Then nobody."

She turned back to the sink, closing the conversation; then she turned back, looking at him.

"Look, Jack, about yesterday in your office—"

"Forget it, Terry."

Her gaze didn't waver. "No. I don't want to forget it. I did it because I wanted to."

Paine looked at her, watched the battle on her face, the decision being made there.

"I want you to know he's gone for me, Jack. He's dead. And if what I did means anything to you, I want you to know it's all right. We can take it from there. I know how hard it would be, but I don't care. It will take time, but I don't care about that, either. The girls would be all right, after a while." She turned back to her dishes. "I know how bad things have been for you, too. I know what you've gone through. There was a time when I almost hated you, because the two miscarriages came while Bobby was helping you out, when he was the only one on the force who stuck his neck out for you. I was wrong. Most of that, the tension, was Bobby, the way he did things. He doesn't back down from anything. I just want you to know it would be all right. I think I could come to love you, Jack."

Paine looked at his coffee; he looked up to see Melissa standing in the doorway, staring at him. She had the eyes of her mother, and she didn't smile.

He opened his mouth to say something, but once again Melissa looked at her mother and then turned and was gone. Somewhere in the back of the house the television set was snapped off in midsentence.

Paine got up and said quietly, "I've got to go, Terry."

$\triangledown$

18

THE POLICE HAD NOT been through Jim Coleman's house yet. Paine wondered if they had found Coleman; for a brief moment, the image of that surprised face staring down from the shower head broke through Paine and made him nauseous.

It was easy to get in; like most cops, Coleman believed in his own invincibility more than in security devices, and, after Paine pulled his gloves on, a cut screen on the side near the back, unseen from the street and well concealed by bushes, was all that was needed.

Coleman's wife had left him long ago, and the house looked as though a single man lived in it. The beam of Paine's flashlight showed wallpaper a woman had obviously chosen still covering the walls in the bedroom, but there was nothing else feminine about it. The bed was unmade, shoes in sloppy ranks along the sideboard where Coleman had dropped them from his feet. A television on the dresser was angled toward the bed, a squeeze of aluminum foil helping the bent rabbit ears on top. It was tuned to Channel 11, the Yankees network; Paine doubted if it had been changed in months.

Washed clothes were stuffed in the dresser, unfolded, with unmatched socks mixed in with underwear. There was nothing else in the drawers. Under the bed there was dust and a couple of *Playboy* magazines. On the floor of the closet, more magazines, some of them hard-core; a box containing porno novels with a mix of mystery novels, and, surprisingly, a couple of history paperbacks: Carl Sandburg's biography of Abraham Lincoln, Bruce Catton's Civil War books. A few shirts hung in the closet, two pair of slacks with empty pockets.

The living room was a mess—open potato chip bags on the scratched coffee table, which was propped up on one end by an old paint can. One good end table, the other a couple of stacked milk crates with an ugly fat lamp on top. A *New York Post* opened to the sports page next to the lamp. A couch between the end tables, a chair with a torn seat next to it, both facing another television, an old color console, against the far wall. Another pair of rabbit ears, newer, again with aluminum foil. A *TV Guide* on top of the TV, two weeks old.

There was nothing for Paine in the living room, nothing in the dining room. A hutch, well preserved but dusty, which stood out against the rest of the furniture: a dining room table and three chairs with worn fabric on the seats, a pile of mail on the table, all junk. On the wall next to the hutch, a wooden case containing a collection of miniature die-cast '50s automobiles.

One of the drawers in the hutch was pulled out. It was empty. Paine went through the rest of them, found nothing: old candles, mail, letters from a brother wanting money. He looked at the open drawer again.

He searched the kitchen, found nothing, backed down the hall and stopped at the bathroom. He pointed the flashlight in.

On the floor, next to the toilet, was a low flat rectangular box, the kind department stores giftwrap shirts in.

Paine went in, picked the box up. He walked back to the living room, sat down on the couch and opened the box, holding the flashlight with his chin, pointing down.

On the top, a three-by-five photograph, four marines bunched together, staring at the camera half solemnly. They shared a comradely look of purpose; one of them on the end, the man Paine and Billy Rader had found beheaded in Fort Worth, smiled grimly.

Next to him was Jim Coleman.

On the other end was Bob Petty.

Paine looked through the rest of the box; there was nothing to do with Vietnam, only the usual valuable papers. It looked as though they had been rifled through, turned aside, until two-thirds of the way down, where Paine imagined the photograph had resided until Coleman had dug it up. The papers around that spot were very old.

On the top of the pile was a ledger book marked Hermano. Paine went through it, found a beautifully neat record of Coleman's dealings that Bryers would love.

Paine put the photograph in his pocket, put the ledger book back in the gift box, closed it, then put the box into the open drawer of the hutch and closed it. He went through the rest of the house, found nothing, went back to the bedroom, turned off his flashlight, and let himself out through the broken screen and went home.

▽

19

WHEN THE TELEPHONE RANG, Paine was in the bad dream, searching for Rebecca between the stars. But she was not there. He was calling for her, his voice loud on a dark, lonely hillside, but the stars were mute until he heard a voice that he thought was hers. But it was the telephone, and he woke up.

"Jack," a voice on the other end of the receiver said when he put it to his ear. He looked at the red digital numbers on the clock next to his bed. It was 3:04 in the morning.

The voice made Paine come fully awake.

"Bobby."

"How are you?" There was something in the voice Paine had never heard in Petty's voice before, a hard calm laced with something that sounded like spite.

"I've been waiting for you to call, Bobby."

Petty chuckled dryly. "I bet you have. I've had you hopping, haven't I?"

"You have, Bobby." Paine was searching for something truly false in the voice—the effects of alcohol, coercion, drugs—and found only chilling, clean directness.

Again Petty chuckled.

"What the fuck is going on, Bobby?"

"Nothing special, Jack. I've just made a change in my life. That's all." Chilling, spiteful directness.

"Why?"

"You were a cop, Jack. You know there are always reasons."

"What are they?"

"That's not something I want to get into. But I think you should forget about finding me. It would be better for everyone."

"Why?"

"Reasons, Jack." Calm, cold. "I realize that you're too fucking stupid to do that, though."

"Terry wants me to quit, but I don't want to."

"Why not? She told you, I'm telling you. It's none of your fucking business."

"It is."

Passion tempered spite. "Because we were friends? Grow up. That was another fucking life. People die. Sometimes they die while they're still alive. And when they get reborn, they're somebody else."

"I don't believe that."

"Believe it. I'm not the Bob Petty you knew, Jack. He's dead and buried." The voice became wishful. "I don't know if he ever existed. I think a long time ago he did. . . ." Petty paused. "I know he did. He was a little boy, and he believed in a lot of things, and that was me, Jack. That was the me you knew." The voice had hardened again. "So give it up, Jack."

"I won't."

"Because we were friends? Because Terry wanted you to? How is Terry, Jack?"

Paine said nothing.

"I want to tell you some things, Jack. And these are no lies. I despised you for a long time, and didn't even know why. But now I do. It's because you're weak, Jack. You were weak when you drank, and you were weak when you tried to kill yourself. You were weaker when you couldn't do it. You know damn well what I'm saying is true. A lot of other people told you these things, but I never did because I felt sorry for you. You were the puppy the kid brings home and hides in his room. Nobody wanted you, Jack, so I took you on.

"Well, I was weak to do that. Your old man put a bullet in his head because he couldn't take what he did, what he felt he had to do, and you're just like him, Jack. Only you don't even have the guts to take yourself out. And I despise you for that.

"When all that shit came down before you got suspended, I was the only one who stood up for you because I knew you couldn't gut it out yourself. That wasn't friendship, Jack. It was pity."

"You're hitting some good buttons, Bobby, but I still don't understand why you left."

"You still don't get it?" Petty's voice rose. "I'm dead, Jack. Dead and gone. There isn't any more Bob Petty like you knew him. That fucking family of mine, you, that job, *it's all dead.* None of it is alive for me anymore."

"What does the word 'tiny' mean, Bobby?"

There was a pause. "You get that from Coleman?"

"Yes."

Petty laughed, the sound of a man who doesn't care. "It doesn't matter."

"Where are you now, Bobby?"

"Listen to me." Petty's voice had softened a little. "I want you to know that I don't care about Terry. I mean that. Whatever happens with her is fine with me. The girls, too. They can do whatever they want. If Terry and you—"

"Tell me where you are."

Petty laughed harshly. "All right, Jack. Sure. If that's what you want."

Petty laughed again, and then the phone went dead in Paine's ear.

Paine called a number, got nothing, called another and let it ring a long time. Finally, someone picked it up. Paine could almost hear the cold stars singing to him.

"Billy?"

"Jack, I tried your office before, left another message."

"You have something?"

"Sure. He's in Tucson. Left New York this morning. No connecting flight."

"I need you for something else. You got anybody who can get armed forces records?"

"What do you need?"

Paine told him about the picture of Paine, Coleman, and Johnson. "There was one other, they looked like a unit. Everything you can get."

"Sure." Rader paused. "Tell you what. I'll meet you tomorrow at a special place in Tucson. You know where I mean?"

"I know where, Billy. Two o'clock?"

"Let me get back to the scope, Jack. Never should have put a phone in here."

"See you tomorrow, Billy."

$\triangledown$

20

CIRCLING IN TO TUCSON AIRPORT, he could not locate Kitt Peak, and soon gave up, concentrating on the beautiful dry city itself, nestled into the sandy mountains of lower Arizona like a solitary desert bird. Tucson was like no other place he had ever been. From the air it looked lonely, an earth city set in an alien landscape of brown, dry mountains and desert bluff; from the ground, it was transformed into a Disney version of any other American city—clean, wide, with the same stores as any other city but under a clear blue wide sky.

The sky, he knew, was not quite so clean, because once he left Tucson behind in his rented Ford and began to climb into the dry summer heat of the mountains, sloping up gently through cactus fields and Indian towns, the orange haze that covered Tucson like a bowl became evident.

From the top of Kitt Peak, the ancient sacred Indian mountain that held eight of the largest telescopes in the world at 7,000 feet, Tucson was only a hazy brown memory forty miles away.

Paine was early. He parked the Escort and wandered down to the solar telescope. There was a tour just going in, and he joined it.

Down into the bowels of the mountain, 700 feet, and into a small dark room. Above them, the odd white tube of the Heliostat let in the burning harsh light of the sun and let it fall onto a large white table, where they watched an image of the solar disk covered with groups of sunspots, each a black magnetic pimple.

There was a short film in a nearby room, the sun flaring before him, throwing long tendrils of white-hot gas from its surface into space. Paine watched it, ever fascinated by the violence of the seemingly benign yellow disk that lit and warmed our planet, and barely felt the hand on his shoulder.

He turned, seeing Billy Rader's bearded smile in the near darkness.

"Howdy," Rader said, but some of his usual effusiveness was gone.

"What's wrong, Billy?"

"Later."

When the film ended, they filed out of the cold shaft of the solar telescope and up into real sunlight "What is it?" Paine asked.

"Plenty of time for that," Billy said. "Let's look at the rest of the scopes."

They went first to the 108-inch telescope, a massive squat tube, the largest on the mountain. Paine and Rader stood regarding it from a galley, separated from the telescope by a flat plate of glass.

"Not like MacDonald Observatory in west Texas, hey, Jack?" Rader said, putting his hand on the glass. "They let you go right up and touch the sucker there."

"And they've got cops like Landers in Texas, too."

Rader laughed. "Ole Landers has got problems right now, Jack. Somebody said something earthshaking to him yesterday, and he up and took a long leave of absence." Rader laughed. "Probably be working at the Motor Vehicle Department when he gets back."

Paine said, "You've got that much power down there, Billy?"

Rader looked at him levelly. His face became serious. "Not really, Jack. It's just who you know. I know a lot of people. Too many. Sometimes I can't do anything at all."

"What happened?"

Rader smiled, but his eyes stayed flat. "Little while, Jack. Let's see the rest."

They saw the other telescopes, the sixty-inch used for

planetary research, the relatively small thirty-inch. Billy insisted on stopping at the gift shop, and bought a dark blue T-shirt with the Andromeda galaxy spread across the front that said Kitt Peak National Observatory on it, along with some postcards. "Got a great telescope postcard collection," he explained. "Come on, let's go look at the scenery."

They moved away from the other tourists, down a sloping stone path to the edge of the cliffs that gave them a panoramic view of Arizona below them. The air was thin and dry, the scene magnificent—wide, flat desert plains dotted with mountain ledges, purple ridges of rock to the far and beautifully bleak horizon.

"No getting away from the heat, eh, Jack? But if you gotta have heat, this is the kind you want. A hundred degrees, but dry as a bone."

"Sure, Billy."

Billy Rader found a seat on one of the cliffs and sat down, dangling his feet over the edge. Paine stood beside him and looked down; there was only a drop of about fifty feet before a second slim ledge fell off a thousand feet below.

"You *like* sitting like that, Billy?"

"Shit, yeah. Makes me feel like God. Even if I am an asshole."

"What happened, Billy?"

"Well," Rader said, scratching his beard, looking at the vista spread below him, "what happened is I can only do so much, Jack. What happened is that I can't help you anymore."

"Why not?"

Rader stared out at nothingness, then suddenly spit out into it. "Because I can't."

"That's the best you can do?"

"We all do our best, Jack. I almost didn't even come today. Yesterday I got my buddy in the Pentagon out of bed and made him sit in front of his computer and tap a few codes in. He was only too happy to do that, considering the poker money he's owed me for five years. So far, so good. Then he calls me back early this morning, and—" Rader looked up at

Paine, the flat look back in his eyes "—he tells me a couple of things and then tells me to forget them."

Paine looked down at him and waited.

Billy Rader stood up, stretched, and turned his back on the spread of Arizona before them. He stared at the high white dome of the 108-inch telescope. "I think you should go home, Jack, go back to fishing. Better yet, come back to Texas with me and look at the sky. We could drive out to MacDonald Observatory."

"What did your man tell you, Billy?"

"I'm not going to tell you, Jack. For a couple of reasons. One of them is I like you a lot. The other is, I like me a lot."

Paine said, "Did he tell you anything?"

"Oh, he told me, all right. Because he's stupid, and thought he'd be paying off that bet. I guess he did. What he did was break national security."

Paine waited.

Rader looked at him closer. "You're not going to quit, no matter what?"

"No matter what."

"All right, then, I'll tell you this much. Your friend Bobby did some very bad things in a place called Cambodia."

Paine waited, unblinking.

"Shit, Jack," Rader said suddenly. He looked at the sky, at the telescope, at Arizona beyond the cliffs. "You won't go home, forget about it?"

"No."

Rader sighed. "Maybe this will help. You knew I'd tell you, anyway." He looked at Paine. "Looks like your friend's going around the mountain. Seems he thought he was doing his business in Cambodia for the old red, white, and blue, but in fact his little covert operation was unauthorized." Rader's stare was trying to make Paine give up. "Looks like he couldn't handle that, Jack, knowing he did the wrong thing for the wrong reason."

"Thanks, Billy."

"Jesus Christ! Don't you see the big picture? Mr. Clean

Marine found out he was dirty and couldn't take it! That's all there is!"

"Maybe," Paine said.

"What are you going to do now?"

"Find out why he's in Tucson."

"Christ!" Rader stomped his foot like an angry horse, looked back at Paine. He reached into his pocket, took out a slip of paper.

"Here," he said, handing it to Paine.

Paine looked at it; on it was a name and address.

Billy Rader said quietly, "That's the other guy in his unit. My friend at the Pentagon gave it to me."

"Thanks."

"You're an asshole, Jack." Rader began to walk away. "I'm gonna have me another look at that big telescope, then I'm going home. If you want anything, don't call me."

He stopped, turned and smiled. "Go ahead and call me, Jack."

"I will, Billy."

21

THE ADDRESS TURNED OUT to be a jewelry store on the edge of Tucson, an ornate little house at the end of a cluster of houses that stood out because there was a sign over the front door that said, Enrique Quinones, Jeweler, and because the house itself was painted turquoise blue. The trim was painted in silver, which made the place look like a large, square piece of Indian jewelry.

When Paine asked for Quinones inside, saying, "Bob Petty sent me," the woman he asked, a walking advertisement for the place, with black hair pulled back and knotted, dark skin, almond eyes, Indian turquoise jewelry around her neck and on her ears and hands, said, "Sure, wait a minute," and went into the back. Paine stood in what should have been the living room, but which had been turned into a showroom, with glass cases, wall shelves with fluorescent lighting above them, a counter with a cash register, Navajo rugs on the floor. Easy listening music floated out from speakers behind the counter. An air conditioner purred softly in one window. Paine smelled Chinese food cooking somewhere in the back of the house.

Quinones came out, holding a .44 Magnum at arm's length pointed at Paine. "Into the back," he said.

Paine went in front of him, down a short hallway past the kitchen, where the saleswoman stood in the doorway looking at the two of them with alarm. Behind her, on the stove, a wok loaded with vegetables steamed.

"Go out front, Maria, and take care of things," Quinones said.

"But—"

"Just go."

She went, slowly, looking back at them.

"Keep walking," Quinones said to Paine.

They passed a bathroom, a closed door, a linen closet. At the end of the hallway was an open door into a dim room and Quinones pushed Paine ahead of him into it.

There was a chair by the far window, and Quinones turned Paine, frisked him, then sat him down in it. "Don't move your hands," he said. "Keep them on your lap or I'll blow your head off."

Paine said, "You like Chinese food?"

"Shut up," Quinones said, and then he jerked his hand forward, raising the butt of the Magnum, and hit Paine hard on the side of the head.

When Paine came back, he heard voices. He was on a low cot or mattress on the floor, on his side, his hands tied behind him, trussed to his bound feet. It was almost dark. The side of his head he had been hit on faced the mattress, and it hurt.

Someone snapped a light on in the next room, and Paine saw the outline of light around the door. He heard voices through the door, muffled but audible.

"Why don't you just go away?" Quinones was saying. He sounded scared.

There was a laugh, which sounded like Bob Petty's. "Sure," was Petty's reply.

"I don't like it," Quinones said.

Petty laughed again, a sardonic sound. "What choice do you have? You always were piss-kneed, Quinones."

"That was all so long ago. . . ."

"To me, it seems like yesterday."

"I just want it all to go away."

"That's not an option, Quinones."

"Please—"

"Just do what I say."

"Tiny—"

Petty's voice grew angry. "Shut up."

"What about your friend?"

"I'll take care of that."

The two voices stopped. Paine heard footsteps approaching his door. A key rattled metallically in the lock, and the door opened. An outline stood there, in front of weak light. The door closed, leaving Paine and the figure in the darkness.

"You just don't know when to quit, do you, Jack?"

"You taught me, Bobby."

"Maybe I did."

Paine heard Petty feeling along the wall, and then a low-wattage light came on across the room. Everything looked sour yellow.

Petty came and stood over him. He was big and square, and looked more solid than ever. The sleeves of his shirt, a dark green one unlike the ones Paine had found in his closet, were rolled up. He leaned down closer and Paine tried to look into his eyes. In the bad light it was like looking into a face of stone. The eyes were like flat marble in a marble face.

"I hope you quit after this, Jack," Petty said flatly, and then he hit Paine in the face with the hard front of his fist and then hit him again.

Paine tried to move, to get out of the way of the blows, but there was nowhere to go. Petty hit him expertly in the face and the ribs and kidneys. Paine felt like a slab of meat on a butcher's table. After a while, to dull the hurt, he tried to detach his mind, to think of himself as a dead block of meat that he was examining from a distance.

Petty didn't speak, but went about his work methodically. After what seemed like days, from a receding place, Paine heard Petty grunting with exertion. Paine's left eye was nearly closed, but he looked up and saw that Petty was sweating. Petty paused for a moment to catch his breath before going to work again.

After what must have been years, Paine saw that the piece of meat on the butcher's block that was himself was in very bad shape, and he could no longer detach himself from that poor slab of beef and it became himself again and he heard himself cry out with each blow.

And then Petty stopped his work, and the heaving catch of breath and the crying that Paine had become was the only sound in the room, until he heard Petty say flatly, "I hope you realize I mean it now, Jack," before the room and the world got very dark and went away.

When Paine came back to consciousness there was a hint of light in the room from the next door. Daylight, perhaps, or a light on in a farther room. Paine managed to turn himself on the bed. His head, his body, hurt terribly. He lay on the mattress for a few moments, willing the throb in the slab of meat that was his body to subside, and finally it did to the point where he could move.

He tried to move into a sitting position but could not. Instead, he arched his back, grabbing his feet with his hands, and began to explore the knot Quinones had made.

It was good, but if he had remembered better, he would have put another loop into the truss that would have made it impossible for Paine to get out of it. But he didn't do that, and after a while Paine had loosened one noose around one foot enough to slip the foot out. The other foot followed. Fifteen more minutes and he had loosened his hands and rubbed blood back into them.

He sat up on the bed.

His body began to throb again. He sat perfectly still, letting the ache do its work.

Finally, he stood, again letting his head have its way, and walked to the door.

It was locked, but it was a cheap bathroom lock and a half minute with his penknife released it.

He eased the door open.

There was still night darkness in the house. The light

came through an open door at the far end of the room he had entered. It was a storage room, boxes of silver chains and clasps, plastic bags of turquoise stones. Boxes filled with white cardboard gift boxes.

Paine went into the outer room, slowly, delicately, painfully.

He was in the cellar of the house. Basement windows showed blackness from outside. There was a workshop, a lathe, a drill press, racks of jewelers' tools on pegboards hung on the walls. A single overhead bulb with a pull chain was on by the stairs.

Paine stepped on the stairs and smelled blood.

The door was open at the top; Paine saw more light in a hallway. As he approached the top the smell of blood was very strong.

An arm lay on the floor across the opening into the cellar, the hand palm up. It wasn't attached to anything.

Paine stepped over it, and saw that the hallway was littered with human limbs.

He found their heads in the living room of the house, the showroom. They were on the sales counter by the cash register, facing one another. The woman's long black hair had been carefully curled around the neck; her earrings did not dangle, two long ovals of turquoise on silver hangers resting on the counter. Quinones's head regarded her; it looked as though his left eye were staring at her earrings.

Paine went to the front door. It was open, warm desert night air filtering into the shop. The moon was up, waxing toward full; the outside world looked nearly as dreamlike as the inside of the jewelry store.

Perhaps because it all looked like a dream, or perhaps because he was getting used to it, or getting angry, this time Paine did not vomit.

$\triangledown$

22

FROM THE ELEVATOR, PAINE could tell that the door to his hotel room was open. He stepped back into the elevator car, waited for the doors to close, and pushed the button for the lobby. The elevator went down and let him off.

He went to the desk, smiled. The nightman smiled back, ignoring the battered face.

"Hi," Paine said. "I'm in 417. Could you tell me if my friend checked in yet? He's supposed to be in the room next to me, but I don't know if that's 415 or 419."

The nightman checked his book. "Would that be Mr. Chambers in 415?"

Paine frowned. "I thought for sure he said 419."

"Room 419 is vacant, sir. Would that be Mr. Chambers?"

"Sure," Paine said, moving away. "Thanks."

Paine went to the end of the lobby, pushed through the glass doors into the pool area, and went to the far end. An old man was in the pool, doing slow laps in dog paddle. He didn't look up as Paine went by.

Paine pushed through to the outside. His room was in the rear, facing the parking lot. The lot was empty.

Paine climbed the fire escape to the fourth floor. There were balconies, and he made his way to the balcony outside room 419.

There was a sliding glass door, which took Paine a few minutes to get through.

He went into the room, slid the door closed behind him. He walked to the bathroom, took a glass tumbler from its sterile wrapper, went into the bedroom and sat on the bed. He put the glass open end to the wall over the bed and put his ear to the other end.

There was silence in the room next door, then a yawn.

"Shit," someone said in a hard whisper.

"Be quiet," a second voice said. "You've been complaining for two hours."

"Doesn't this fucker ever sleep? I'm hungry."

"You'll eat when we're finished."

"I'm hungry now."

"You should have brought something."

"I ate it an hour ago.

"Just be fucking quiet."

"It's uncomfortable, too. These chairs are uncomfortable."

The other one sighed loudly. "This is the last time I work with you, Martin."

Martin laughed. "You think I complain too much? Tell Gordon to transfer you. Fine with me, Sims."

"You did nothing but—"

"You hear something?" Martin said in a fierce whisper.

"I said shut up!"

There was silence; Paine heard someone walk by in the hallway outside, whistling. After a moment he heard the elevator doors open and then close. The whistling went away.

"Wasn't him," Martin said. "Where the hell is he?"

"Will you be quiet?"

"I told you I was hungry and uncomfortable. These chairs are uncomfortable."

Paine pulled the glass away from the wall, set it down on the table next to the bed. He picked up the phone, dialed room 417.

The phone rang awhile. Paine could imagine them arguing in the dark as to whether to pick it up or not. Finally, one of them did.

"Sims?" he said purposefully. "Gordon told me to tell you

we've got him spotted across the street at the Marriott. Go downstairs. Tell Martin to wait outside the door, in the hallway. You hear me?"

Sims started to protest, but Paine said, "Gordon says now," and hung up the phone.

Paine went to the door and waited. There was a commotion next door, then the door opened and someone strode to the elevator, got on it, and was gone.

Paine opened the door, stepped out into the hallway, pretended to lock his own door. He walked quickly by Martin, standing in the hallway, turned and punched Martin in the face.

"Hey!" Martin protested, but Paine pushed him back through the door into his hotel room, punched him again, kicked the door closed behind him. Martin was feeling around his chest under his jacket, so Paine planted his fist in Martin's groin and Martin went down to the rug groaning. Paine pushed him back with his foot and went through Martin's jacket, coming up with a snub-nosed .38 in a shoulder holster. He put the gun to Martin's nose.

"Talk very clearly," Paine said, the adrenaline rush masking the pain that had flared when he'd punched Martin.

Martin was still groaning, so Paine made a deeper impression on Martin's nose with the barrel of the gun until Martin's eyes focused on him.

Paine said, "Are you FBI?"

Martin shook his head no.

"Who?"

"DEA."

"Bullshit," Paine said. He pushed the circle of steel harder into the side of Martin's nose. "Where's your ID?"

"Inside pocket, right side," Martin said.

Paine kept pressure on the gun, and reached into the jacket pocket opposite the holster. There was an ID there, identifying Raymond Martin, special agent, Drug Enforcement Agency.

"What the fuck are you doing in my hotel room?" Paine said.

Martin became silent.

"Tell me or I'll put another fucking nostril in your nose," Paine said.

"Waiting to talk to you."

"About what?"

"You're obstructing a drug investigation."

Paine pressed the gun hard into Martin's nose, waiting for more.

"We're looking for Robert Petty."

"Why?"

Martin became silent again.

Paine was going to threaten him again when he saw Martin's eyes focus from Paine to something behind him, and Paine felt the end of the barrel of someone else's .38 in his neck.

"Drop the gun, get up, put your hands on your head," Sims's voice said behind Paine.

Paine did what he was told.

Martin got up and smiled at Sims, who was nearly as heavy as Martin but wore the weight better. He was balding and wore rimless glasses and didn't smile.

"Does this mean we can eat?" Martin said cheerfully, pulling Paine's hands down behind his back to handcuff them.

"Just shut up, okay?"

Martin finished with the cuffs then came around to stand next to Sims and look at Paine. "He said he was going to put another nostril in my nose," Martin said, looking hurt.

Sims said to Paine, "You're in a bunch of trouble, shithead. 'Course it looks like someone already told your face that."

"Did you have a warrant to break into my hotel room?" Paine said, ignoring the comment. He wanted to lie down. Or die.

Sims smirked, taking two folded pieces of paper out of his pocket. "That, and another birthday surprise. I have a war-

rant for your arrest for the murder of somebody named . . ."
He unfolded the paper and read from it. ". . . James Coleman, of Yonkers, New York." He smiled. "You're going back
to New York, cop killer."

Martin smiled at Paine, turned to Sims. "Can we eat now,
Jerry?" he asked.

▽

23

CHIEF BRYERS, WITH HIS car and driver, was waiting for Paine at LaGuardia Airport. As they pulled away from Sims and Martin, who had personally flown back with Paine and who stood smiling and waving at the curb outside the American Airlines terminal, Bryers removed Paine's handcuffs.

"Relax," Bryers said. "You're not being charged with anything."

Paine looked at him levelly; there seemed to be a hint of amusement on Bryers's face behind the bureaucrat's veneer. "Then what am I doing here?"

"There was a time, for about twenty minutes yesterday, when you were directly connected with the murder of Jim Coleman."

"Who issued the warrant?"

Bryers smiled slightly. "I did. Let's just say I was politely asked to do it."

"By who?"

"The U.S. Attorney's office. And let's say he was asked by someone else above him."

"You were ordered to have me sent back to New York?"

Bryers said, *"Asked."* The chagrined smile remained.

"Don't you care about being jerked around?" Paine asked.

Bryers's demeanor darkened. "That's not the way I'd put it."

"How would you put it?"

"Let's just say a lot has happened since yesterday. A lot of it I have you to thank for."

Paine waited for more.

Bryers suddenly smiled widely and slapped Paine on the knee. "You're a good man, Jack. You're honest, and you're tough. I'd like you to work for me."

"Didn't Coleman make me an unauthorized job offer a few days ago?"

"This is different. You've helped me clean up the whole department in less than a week, and I'd like to have you around for good. Rank of detective, second class, to start. We can talk about salary over drinks."

Paine studied Bryers's face to see if he was joking. But Bryers didn't have the kind of face that joked.

Bryers said, "Don't you realize what you've done?"

"No."

"You did break into Coleman's house, didn't you? You left no prints but I know it was you."

After a moment, Paine said, "Yes."

"You didn't plant that stuff in the hutch drawer, did you?"

"It was there already."

Bryers almost laughed. "Well, don't you realize that Coleman's log contained the names of every crooked cop in the department, and half the dealers in Yonkers? That would have taken me months, maybe years, to get at. I've got ten indictments already, and another five in the works! And then the department's *clean!*"

"That's nice."

"Jack, in twenty years, I've never had a day like this! We even solved Roberto Hermano's murder." He laughed. "Turned out it was a lover's quarrel, if you want to call it that. Hermano was a fag. Apparently he and some other fag named Philly Ramos were an item. When Roberto started fooling around on the side with a sixteen-year-old named Jeff Samuels, Ramos found out about it and killed him out of jealousy. This kid Samuels came to us with his parents. They were white as a sheet, their little boy, good background, all-white school, mixed up with this kind of homo crap. The kid was a wreck, told us everything. He said Bob Petty had

been protecting Hermano, and that after Petty disappeared
Roberto wanted to leave New York with Samuels, but the kid
wouldn't go with him." Bryers's enthusiasm dropped a notch.
"Jack, I *am* sorry about your friend Petty turning out bad—"

"Who said Petty was involved?"

"His prints were all over the club where we found
Coleman's body. So were yours. You tell *me* what to think."

"Was his name in Coleman's ledgers?"

"No. But he and Coleman could have had a separate
agreement. Or Petty may have gone on the take recently. Or
maybe Petty decided to take over the whole operation."

Paine was silent.

"Look, Jack, you have to be reasonable," Bryers said. "I've
got Petty directly connected with a murder in Yonkers, one
in Fort Worth, Texas, and now I have an APB in from Tucson
for Petty for the murder of someone named Enrique Quinones and his girlfriend. All of the bodies were hacked to
pieces and decapitated. I think it's safe to say that Petty is
involved, and that he may be out of his mind. What do you
think? Of course, you were there, too. And you look like you
were in a war. So talk to me."

"I don't know what to think."

"Listen, Paine," Bryers said. "I'd really like you to come
back to the department. It would be good for you, for me, for
everyone."

"How would it be good for me?"

Bryers showed surprise. "Don't you miss the police force?
Your father was a good cop, from what I hear."

"I don't miss the force."

Bryers's surprise increased. "Do you mean that?"

"Look," Paine said, facing Bryers, letting anger run into
his face. "I was a cop once, I was in love with it then, but
I'm not a cop anymore."

"But with all the corruption gone—"

"The way I see it, this is your way of keeping the feds
happy by putting a lid on me. You know if you charge me
with Coleman's murder I'll be out in six hours."

Bryers just looked at him. "There's something else. The U.S. Attorney's office informed me that they're investigating a government leak they think breached national security."

Paine said nothing.

"It's serious stuff," Bryers continued. "They told me five to ten, just for being involved. They'd really like to find the leak."

"All I want to do is find out what happened to Bob Petty."

Bryers suddenly became very formal. He turned away from Paine, staring straight out through the glass partition, through the windshield of the car. "I'm afraid I can't let you do that. Part of the deal I made with the U.S. Attorney's office was that you stay in New York."

"You made the deal, I didn't."

"It's not that simple. If you try to leave New York, I'll have to arrest you for Coleman's murder."

"But you told me—"

"That's right. I told you. But I didn't say it was official. Officially, for the sake of the U.S. Attorney's office, I let the warrant stand."

"I told you it wouldn't stick."

Bryers was humorless, the bureaucrat again. "They've got a job to do. We all do. Is this your office?"

The car had stopped in front of Paine's building. The driver in front sat unmoving, hands on the wheel, waiting.

Paine said, "Thanks for the ride."

As he was getting out of the car Bryers put his hand on Paine's arm. "Think about my offer." A hint of a clinically friendly smile came back to his face. "Like I said, it would be good for everybody."

"Good for you?" Paine said, and Bryers removed his hand from Paine's arm.

"Everybody," Bryers said, stonily.

Paine got out of the car and closed the door. He watched Bryers make a motion to the driver, and then the car pulled away from the curb and moved off.

24

ALL THE LIGHTS WERE on in Paine's office. The door was open. The air conditioner was on, rattling unsuccessfully in the window, making noise, pushing hot air into the corners of the room.

Anapolos was sitting on Paine's chair, behind his desk, going through his mail.

Paine stood in the doorway and said, "I just got out of Police Chief Bryers's car. You want me to call him back and report a breaking and entering?"

Anapolos looked up at him mildly. "Do what you want, Mr. Paine. We'll let the lawyers settle it. If you read your lease closely, you'll see that I have the right of entrance. I have a key for the premises, and I used it."

"I don't have a lawyer," Paine said. He crossed the room, walked around his desk, and grabbed Anapolos by the shirt-front, yanking him up out of the chair.

Anapolos gasped, his eyes going wide. "Mr. Paine, the lawyers—"

"I told you I don't have a lawyer," Paine said. "I don't need one."

Holding Anapolos tightly by the shirt, Paine danced him back around the desk to the front and dropped him into one of the padded chairs.

"Mr. Paine, Mr. Paine . . ." Anapolos gasped, trying to regain his breath along with his dignity.

Paine sat behind his desk and drew a key from his pocket. Ignoring Anapolos, he fitted the key into the lower right-hand drawer of the desk, unlocked it, opened the drawer, and brought out a portable cassette deck. There was a tape in it, and Paine rewound it.

"Listen," Paine said. He pushed the Play button, and both he and Anapolos listened to Koval and Kohl's antics in Paine's office, the threats, the short fight, Koval's whining announcement that Anapolos had sent them to beat Paine up.

Paine turned off the tape recorder, removed the tape, and put it in his pocket. He rummaged in the back of the open drawer, found a fresh tape, unwrapped it and put it in the machine. He put the recorder back in the drawer, slid it closed, locked it, and pocketed the key.

"Anything to say?" Paine said. "Should I get a lawyer?"

Anapolos began to sputter, "I didn't—I did not send—"

"Here's what you're going to do," Paine said. "And you're going to do it of your own free will. I am not blackmailing you. The tape, which I'm going to copy and send to Chief Bryers, asking him not to open it unless I ask him to, is just something I have in my possession. It has nothing to do with you, unless you want it to. Unless you want lawyers going over it.

"What you're going to do is leave me alone. You're going to draw up a new lease, without the right of entrance clause, and the term of the lease is going to be ninety-nine years. The rent will go up with the rate of inflation each year, which is fair. Also in my new lease will be a clause guaranteeing strict maintenance of my office, at your expense. The office will be painted every five years. You will make sure there are no water leaks, no roaches, no rats, no termites. Also, and this will be the first thing you do, you will make sure that either the air conditioner in here is fixed, immediately, or that a new one is installed.

"Have your lawyer witness the lease, get it notarized, and send it to me. Now get out, Mr. Anapolos."

Anapolos sat unmoving in his chair, struck dumb. "Mr. Paine—"

"I've been nothing but fair, Mr. Anapolos. You're an asshole and I don't like you, and what I should really do is tell Chief Bryers to play the tape I send him as soon as he gets it. He'll like it. He's a stickler for details. He doesn't like corruption, and scumbags like you offend his sense of order.

"What would happen to you is that you would be arrested and booked, and then spend at least a night in jail while your relatives come up with bail. Then you would go to trial and lose, because Koval and Kohl would testify against you after being promised immunity. And you would spend about nine months in jail, during which time you would be fucked in the rear end until your rectum is wide enough to pass a grapefruit."

Paine stopped as Anapolos scurried for the door, closing it gently behind him. "All right, Mr. Paine," he said, and in a moment Paine heard the elevator wheeze him down to the ground.

Paine turned on the answering machine on his desk. He was checking through the blank tape when the phone rang.

When he put the receiver to his ear, Philly Ramos's voice said, "Hello, Paine." The voice sounded faraway, vague, haunted.

"You want me to help you, Philly?"

"I don't think I can be helped, Paine."

"You sure, Philly? I can take you in, make sure the police take care of you."

"I don't think that's possible. Anyway . . ." He laughed, a pained sound. "Remember how Roberto used to say he couldn't stand to go back to jail again?"

"Yes."

Again the hurt laugh. "That was me, Paine. Worse than Roberto. I was only in once, for a few months. But it was enough."

"What are you going to do?"

The laugh. "Doing it now, Paine. Doesn't hurt as much as I thought. Bathwater's all red. . . ."

"Philly, where are you?"

"Forget it, Paine. Too late." The hurt laugh was softening.

"Philly, don't do this, let me help you."

"Sorry, don't need help. Told you I can't go back in. Even for a night. Maybe I know what I like, but I always wanted it nice. I wanted it to be nice for Roberto. But I told you, he played the fence with everybody. Even me. The only time I get mean, Paine, is when somebody doesn't play straight with me."

"Philly—"

"Thanks for talking, Paine. I was going to do it anyway. Just wanted someone to be with me. I could have made it good for you, Paine, nice, better than Roberto. I would have loved you forever, man. . . ."

Philly's voice trailed off to a sigh, and then the phone was hung up in Paine's ear and he heard the final, harsh tone of disconnection.

Paine hung up the phone, then picked it up again to repeat, for a moment, that final sound.

▽

25

IN THIS BAD DREAM, Rebecca would not appear, and Bob Petty refused to change.

Paine was on a high hill, in the dark, with the stars of summer covering him like a bowl. He was alone, and even the distant crickets had ceased their whispering chatter. The world was dark and hot, with the stars unmoving above.

He had a telescope, and he looked for her, but she was not there. He searched between the stars, went over the glowing gas clouds, the thick blanket of suns in the southern Milky Way, up overhead to the deep reaches of black space where the constellation Cygnus ruled. He saw things he had rarely seen: the thin wisp of lace that was the Veil nebula, shining for him with a beauty that should have made him sing. But he was afraid, and he wanted to find her, and she would not appear.

He looked deeper, into the dark spaces, and saw things no man had seen with a telescope. Planets whirled around protostars, stars were born in the midst of fiery clouds of heated gas, glowing with color: red and green, the blue-white of beginning life. His telescope brought him deeper still into the void, where quasars, borning galaxies of remarkable heat and power, rumbled with the beginnings of everything itself. And still he did not see her.

He went farther, his eye glued desperately to the eyepiece. He felt tears on his cheeks in the hot night, mingled with sweat, and he began to call her name. There was an ache in him deeper than the space he explored, a need for solace, and for her to be alive again, that no beautiful sight of God's creation, of nature's beginnings, could put to rest. He sought not the birth of all, but the negation of her extinction. She was gone, and he wanted her back, and the rest of creation was a mere mockery, a beginning that only led to death.

"Rebecca!" he cried, grasping the telescope with both his hands, and now his eye, with the eye of glass that was the telescope, brought him deeper still. He saw the beginning itself, a tiny flash of pure horrible light in the distance, and it filled his vision and blotted out the darkness, and she was not in the heated light, she was nowhere. She was gone.

"Rebecca!" he called, his voice an echo in creation, but she was not there. . . .

And then Bobby Petty was there. His face grew out of the creation, and it filled the lens of his telescope, and creation withdrew behind him, and Paine began to return to his hilltop. He saw everything behind Petty pull back: roaring quasars, the galaxies they made, the protosuns, their planets condensing from hard rock, till the rock became Earth.

And Bob Petty's face was there.

And still he would not change. Still, Bob Petty was himself. And Petty opened his mouth in laughter, only it wasn't laughter that came out but sobs, the crying of the essential self that was deep inside his own self, behind the masks, and Paine suddenly knew that Petty's cold eyes that had looked down at him were false, and that all he had done to his family and his life was false, and that Bobby Petty had not changed after all.

Paine woke up.

He was stiff and bathed in night sweat, but he ignored it and sat on the edge of the bed and punched a number into the telephone. He was not yet awake, and in his mind the night of his dream and the night that Billy Rader in Texas would be looking at were the same. And he saw Billy Rader peering into his telescope, and looking between the stars, and seeing incredible things.

"Billy?" he said.

"Jack? You all right?"

Paine took a few breaths and said, "Yes."

"Shitty night here, Jack. Clouds came in about an hour ago. I was just shutting down. Another five minutes, I would have been on the road back to Fort Worth."

"Billy," Paine repeated, but he still was not fully awake, and he still saw things through the telescope on the hill, though the dream was fading and he heard Billy's voice clearly now.

"Jack," Billy said resignedly. "Hold on while I go out to my car."

"What?"

"Hold on, Jack."

Paine waited, the world coming back to him, the hot room coming back to him, the stale breeze from the fan, the night stagnation, the hot summer.

"I'm back," Billy Rader said. "But you have to promise me something. I'm going to give you something, but I want you to promise me you got this yourself. My friend in the Pentagon almost got his nuts screwed off the other day because of you and me. This time, you have to tell the feds you got it yourself."

Paine said, "I promise."

Billy Rader sighed heavily. "Here it is, Jack. They threatened to can my friend, and he got pissed. He knows people in the White House, he called them, they told him nothing. He threatened whistle-blower, and they got back to him in fifteen minutes and said they'd cover his ass. He's still pissed, Jack."

"About what?"

"They lied to him. The stuff he got out of the computer was a cover. He went deeper, and found a covert operation. A *domestic* covert operation. I think you know what I'm talking about. This thing gets out, it'll be worse than Iran-Contra."

"I'm listening."

Rader sighed again. "Here goes. I've got faxes of two computer printouts here, and, according to them, your friend Bobby Petty was set up."

Paine saw Petty's face, the laughter in the mouth, the sobbing that came out.

Rader went on. "This is what happened. Petty and his friends were an elite operations unit in Vietnam. In 1970, after Nixon became president, they were sent into Cambodia a couple of times. One of those times, on direct orders, so they thought, they wiped out the entire male population of a VC village. What they were told was that the village was a direct ferry route to the Ho Chi Minh Trail, supplying Chinese weapons to Ho's men as they came down.

"When Petty and his boys were led in there, they found a lot of weapons, just like they were told they would. There was a firefight. The women and children they drove out, but they wiped out the male population. All of them. Then they went back to Vietnam, mission completed. Supposedly, a good part of the munitions reaching the Viet Cong on the way down the Ho Chi Minh Trail had been eliminated.

"Only, somebody lied to them. What they were really sent to do was handle a personal vendetta against a Cambodian drug operation that had stiffed someone. That someone was the guy who led Petty's team into Cambodia. His name was Kwan Wac Ho. He was also known as Tiny Man."

"Jesus."

"Yeah," Billy said. "But it gets better. Because Tiny Man has been living in the U.S. since 1973, and has been linked to several drug smuggling operations. Most recently, he's been helping a group of South Americans get set up in a little town you might have heard of in New York, called Yonkers."

"Fuck."

"Yeah again." Rader's voice became sad. "Looks like your friend Bobby found out something he can't live too well with, Jack. Imagine living all that time with the thought that you did a great service for your country, that you saved a lot of American lives by handling a dangerous mission wiping out a village of bloodthirsty Viet Cong sympathizers funneling to their brethren weapons used to kill Americans. Then imagine finding out that you didn't do that after all, that all you did was murder a bunch of poor Cambodians trying to make a buck by shoveling coca weed. Could do some things to your head."

"Yes," Paine said.

"Seems a lot more reasonable him going bonkers over this than over a woman or something else, doesn't it?"

"Yes."

"I'm sorry, Jack, I truly am. Looks like somebody in D.C. found out this guy Tiny Man has been running amok in the drug trade, and with this new drug war and all was afraid that if he got caught the regular way a whole line of dirty old wash would get hung out. I mean, we're talking about another My Lai here, and in Cambodia, yet. So this somebody tells Petty the real story and figures Petty'll go birddog and take care of the whole mess for them. I mean, look at Coleman. Maybe Petty was the only one who didn't know why they went into Cambodia. It could happen, couldn't it?"

Paine didn't want to say it. He saw Petty's face before him, the laughing face filled with tears, and he saw the essential Bobby Petty, the blue soul deep inside him that had found that his heroism had turned to shit, that he was a murderer as much as any man he had ever tracked, and that his family and friends would, from this time onward, know only a murderer and would be tainted by his presence just as his own soul was tainted, and that he could never look into their eyes again without seeing his own sin reflected in them, and in their lives. And Paine saw the essential Bob Petty and knew that he would wipe his family and friends free of him, separate them in reality even as they were separated by sin, and he saw Bob Petty coldly doing all these things out of love—the destruction of his family, the alienation of his friends, the renunciation of his livelihood. Paine now saw Petty's face not in a dream but in reality, in that room as Petty stood over him with the cold eyes not of hate but of self death, of love, as Petty swung his fist up, the tremble in the fingers, and brought it down upon Paine as a loving kiss. . . .

"Jack, couldn't it happen?"

Paine saw Petty's face and wanted to believe that he couldn't go mad, could not execute his fellow murderers as they had executed a village of innocent men in an alien country, but Paine knew that this was something that was part of Bob Petty's essential self—was, in fact, part of his own and most other men's—for madness is sometimes the handmaiden of justice.

"Jack?"

"Yes," Paine whispered, "it could happen."

The line between them was silent a long time. Paine heard the hiss in the wires, the distance of a wire in the ground and hung on a pole, the wire connecting his mind, his soul, to Billy Rader's mind and soul, and, finally, Billy Rader said what he had to.

"I'm going to write about this thing, Jack. You know I have to. When it's all over, when I have everything in place, I'm going to publish it. Too many people will be hurt if I don't. It's too big a story to let go. We're talking about another big government scandal, something that shouldn't be going on. All of us get burned when that happens." His voice became quieter. "I know what will happen to your friend, and I'm sorry."

"I know," Paine said.

There was another silence. And then Billy Rader said, "There's one other thing, which I know you would find out anyway. I don't want you ever to think I'm using you, Jack, that it's for a story. It's just that I know you, and you'd find it out anyway."

"Go ahead, Billy."

"I just want you to be careful, Jack. I want you to be very careful."

"I will."

"I know where Bobby is now, where Tiny Man must be."

And then he told Paine where.

26

PAINE DIDN'T LIKE WEARING disguises. When he had used the drinking glass to listen in on Sims and Martin, it had made him feel as if he were playing detective. But there were times when playing detective worked, and was necessary. He had colored his hair blond, and he wore a red baseball cap, and he had a blond mustache called "the Baron" that he had ordered from an outfit in New York that supplied Broadway theaters, and he wore an old denim jacket and a pair of faded jeans with the bottoms frayed, and an old pair of sneakers. All of these things together made him look like someone else, a guy from Yonkers who worked on the crew that mowed your lawn, perhaps. He looked like someone on a budget heading to Tucson to see a friend, or, perhaps, to try to persuade his errant girlfriend to come back to New York. He didn't look like someone who would succeed in getting the girlfriend to come back, but that was all right.

At La Guardia, he told the ticketseller that his name was Jimmy Plunkett and paid in cash. He smiled a lot. People smiled back, and soon he was on a flight with his headset on, thinking about the fed he had seen hanging around outside his apartment building in Yonkers. He knew the disguise was all right, and the makeup covering the bruises, because he had gone up to the fed and asked him the time, smiling, and the fed had not smiled but had given him the time and then put his dead eyes back on the front of the building.

"Thanks, man," he had said.

The fed had answered, "Get lost."

The flight was long, and he slept a little, but Bobby Petty didn't haunt his dreams any longer. When he didn't sleep he listened to the headset and stared at the flat earth below and enjoyed the stale air-conditioned atmosphere of the plane until it landed in Tucson, where it was still 100 degrees with no help in sight.

He rented a car, paying cash and showing his Jimmy Plunkett driver's license. He kept smiling, and everyone smiled. When you pay cash, he thought, it didn't matter if you looked like a landscaper's assistant from Yonkers, everyone returned your smile.

He wondered how long it would be before the fed outside his building, and Bryers, and Sims and Martin, found out he was not in Yonkers.

He figured he had twenty-four hours.

He drove past the hotel he had stayed in before, thought of going up to room 419 to see if Martin and Sims were still there and ask them the time. He kept driving.

He drove a long while.

He was almost where he wanted to go when he knew for sure that he was being followed. A tan Datsun had made all of his turns, and he didn't know how long it had been back there but he knew it had gotten closer. He tried to make it get closer still, to see the driver, but it hung back, refusing to bite.

He made a few more turns, getting fancy with the wheel, but the Datsun stayed with him.

Finally, he picked a wide street with lots of light on it and pulled over to the curb.

The Datsun, a half block behind, pulled over and stopped.

Paine got out of his car and began to walk toward the Datsun. The sun was in the windshield, and he still couldn't see the driver. And then, as Paine approached the car, the driver's door opened, and the driver got out.

"Paine," Philly Ramos said, smiling. "What a lousy disguise."

As Paine got close, Philly held out his right hand in greeting. In it was a small can, the top of which he depressed.

A small cloud came out of the can, up into Paine's face.

"Sorry, man," Philly Ramos said, affectionately.

Paine began to choke; his eyes watered and he could not see. He threw out his arms and backed away from Philly Ramos.

But then Philly said, "Sorry," again, with gentleness, and something came down hard on the back of Paine's skull and he met blackness.

27

PAINE AWOKE IN A ROOM somewhere, sitting up on a chair, handcuffed behind. Paine's throat was parched with the taste of chemicals and dry heat.

Philly came into the room and smiled. He wore a long silk paisley robe. His feet were bare. The toenails shone as if they had been covered with clear lacquer. Philly had loosened his ponytail; his straight, ink black hair hung loosely down, framing his beautiful face.

"Good morning, Paine." He smiled. He went to a window in the room, threw open the curtains, and opened the blinds. Hot morning sunlight slatted the room.

"What the hell did you spray me with, Philly?"

Philly's face brightened. "The Israeli army developed it for dealing with Palestinians. You like the bouquet?"

"The shit works."

"Let me get you a cup of coffee to wash that taste out of your mouth." Philly turned and went to another room.

"Where are we?" Paine called after him.

Philly laughed. "A place outside of Tucson. I have friends in the Indian community."

"Are we on a reservation?"

Philly appeared in the doorway with a steaming cup of coffee in one hand. "Yes, Paine, we're on a reservation."

"What the hell is going on, Philly?"

"Don't talk," Philly said, crossing the room to stand before Paine. He leaned down, putting the lip of the coffee cup to Paine's mouth. "Drink."

Paine sipped; his eyes rose and locked on Philly's, studying
his face. Philly's eyes were wise, brown, beautiful pools.

Philly's face pulled back slightly, the eyes still studying.
"I meant what I said about being good to you," he said.

"Why did you lie about killing yourself?"

The eyes stayed solemn above the smile. The mouth
matched the eyes. "I knew you had a weakness for suicides."

"Not anymore."

Philly abruptly stood up, pulling the coffee away. A splash
of it spilled on Paine. A sharpness entered Philly's voice. "It
would have been too late now, anyway."

"You're the South American connection, aren't you,
Philly?"

"That's me," Philly said. "I have the connections in Cen-
tral and South America. I have family, I have friends."

"You told me you were finished with drugs."

"I don't take them anymore," he said. "But when you
want nice things in your life, when you want things to be
nice for the one you love, that takes money, and . . ." He
looked at Paine, brown eyes large. "You find a way to make
money."

"What about Roberto?"

The eyes stayed large, liquid. "Roberto betrayed me."

"With the boy?"

Philly laughed. "There were other boys. They were toys
for Roberto. I wanted things to be nice for Roberto, I wanted
him to have anything he wanted. As long as he let me take
care of him, I didn't care what he did. But he wanted to leave
me, and threatened to tell Petty about me, and that would
have ruined everything."

"Then why were Kwan's boys so upset about Roberto's
murder?"

Philly laughed harshly. "I told you, Roberto used everybody. He had Kwan thinking he was the connection to South
America, that without him nothing could happen." His
large eyes looked sad. "And that's why I followed you from
New York to catch you, Paine. Kwan doesn't like people who

interfere. You're going to help me make him forget about Roberto."

"How?"

"Kwan can use you as bait."

"For what?"

"To catch Bobby Petty."

The day went along. Philly left the house, and Paine was left alone in the room in his chair, feeling the dry heat, watching the bands of hot light on the wall moving down as the sun moved up. Philly had gagged his mouth, and the hot air Paine pulled in through his nose was uncomfortable. Outside, he heard a desert bird call to another desert bird; the second bird didn't want to answer, peeping without enthusiasm, but the first bird kept at it. The cuffs were tight, and Philly was good with knots and Paine could not loosen his feet. His hands went to sleep for a while, and he shook them back awake. In late afternoon he heard two boys walk by the house playing ball, the ball making hard smacking sounds near the window, the boys occluding the bars of light, but the boys kept walking and everything became silent and hot again. In late afternoon, as the slats reached the floor and then faded as the sun moved up over the house, the desert bird called again to his mate, and this time there was an enthusiastic answer and they flew off together, peeping amiably.

Philly returned near nightfall. He entered the house whistling, and when he came into the room he smiled at Paine. He turned on a floor lamp in one corner. He was cradling a long paper bag. He wore an open-necked silk shirt and loose khaki trousers. A single thin silver chain circled his neck, and he wore a tiny silver earring. His hair was pulled back in a ponytail once more.

"Good news, Paine," he said. He came to Paine, put down his paper sack, and untied the gag; Paine felt how soft his fingers were.

"For you or me?"

Philly laughed, picked up the paper bag, and removed a

bottle of wine from it. "You must be thirsty."

He left the room, returning soon with two wineglasses with ice in them. He opened the bottle, and half filled both glasses. He sat down in front of Paine, crossing his legs, and held up one glass in toast.

"To you, Paine."

"What are you toasting?"

"They'll be here in an hour."

"And you?"

Philly rose, lifted the other wineglass, and tilted it so Paine could sip from it. "I go back to Yonkers."

"And work for Kwan?"

"Kwan will have to be quiet in Yonkers for a while, but things will settle down. Everything is set up for him. When he wishes, when the police realize that they must start from the beginning, then he will begin."

"Will he let you retire?"

"He already has." He let Paine finish the wine, put the glass on the floor. He walked to the doorway, stopped, but didn't turn.

"Just so you know," he said, "Roberto didn't suffer."

"You cut his balls off, Philly."

"That was after. I loved him, Paine."

Then he walked out and was gone.

An hour passed, perhaps a little more. Paine heard what sounded like a jeep pass the house, go on, come back. Car doors slammed. The front door of the house was opened, pushed in, hard. Two figures came to the doorway of Paine's room, looked, a third pushed past them into it.

The figure came close to Paine, the black man from the alley next to Paine's office building. He studied Paine closely, put his fingers on Paine's false mustache and tore it off. He turned to his two companions.

"Yes," he said curtly, and they came into the room and lifted Paine from his chair, holding him under the arms, and followed their leader out into the night.

$\triangledown$

28

It was a jeep, like Paine had thought. He had hoped the night air would be cooler, but the desert hadn't given up its heat yet and he continued to sweat. They put him in the back. Paine saw that they were just off the highway in a little settlement of modest houses, dusty yards, chickenwire enclosures, rusted vehicles on blocks. They pulled out on the highway and now Paine knew where they were: between Tucson and Kitt Peak. The stars were out, brushing the sky with tiny lights. Somewhere behind him the domes would be open, searching.

The jeep went fast. When they got nearer to Tucson's glow one of the two followers, at their leader's order, threw a blanket over Paine and the stars went away. It was a wool blanket, and made him sweat more. They rode for what Paine estimated to be another twenty minutes.

Finally, they slowed, curled into a short stretch of road, stopped.

The blanket was lifted; a black face hovered over him.

"Nothing personal, man," the face said, and then the butt end of an AK-47 clubbed him to unconsciousness.

Literally, a padded room. Paine felt himself underground, a dampness ordinarily missing from the desert. It was still hot. He was stripped down to his boxer shorts. He had been thrown on an old mattress in one corner. A single light bulb in the middle of the beamed, insulated ceiling illuminated the blue-padded walls, the white-painted concrete floor. The room was about twenty by twenty feet. There was no stair-case. Except for his mattress, and two dog bowls next to it, one containing water, the other empty, there was nothing in the room.

Paine's head hurt. He drank water from one bowl, uri-nated into the other. An exchange of liquids. There were no basement windows in the room.

Paine was used to waiting, and he waited. His stomach began to ache for food, but none came. His head ached and there was nothing to help that except a month of fishing.

Sometime during the wait he napped; when he awoke it was hotter in the room. Midday. He could almost feel the sun moving overhead, turning the desert into heat haze. Paine sweated freely, watched the sweat take part of his weight away. He finished the water in the bowl, felt no urge to urinate again, wanted more water.

He napped again, fainting, actually, and sometime in the middle of it he was awakened by a sound. A corner of the room opened up, insulated ceiling pulled up and hinged back. A long metal ladder was lowered, rubber feet angling to hard purchase against the painted floor.

One of the black men scampered down the ladder, stopped halfway, waited for a burden that was lowered to him. An-other of the black men came down behind him, and they brought down into the room something long and heavy in a canvas duck sack. They carried it to the far wall and dropped it on the floor. Paine sat up on his mattress but they ignored him, walking back to the ladder and climbing up. The ladder stayed.

Paine rose and was moving to the ladder when the leader of the black men came down it. "Sit on the mattress," he said in a flat voice. His two compatriots followed him down, one bearing a pitcher of water, the other a bowl of fruit—ba-nanas, an apple, two oranges.

They refilled his water bowl and Paine drank half of it; the water had been iced and tasted good. The fruit bowl was put down beside the mattress. Paine ate a banana immediately under the watchful eyes of the black leader; the others stood to either side of Paine, brandishing their weapons.

There came a sound from above, and the black leader immediately took the fruit bowl away from Paine. He handed it to one of the others, who put it out of reach, and as he did this a figure climbed quickly down the ladder. When he turned around and smiled, Paine knew it must be Kwan.

He *was* tiny, perhaps four foot ten or eleven. He wore baggy khaki trousers and a loose T-shirt that had a picture of a bottle of Coca Cola on it. He moved gracelessly, all jerks and angles. His face was wide, flat, and empty, a clean slate with eyes, flat nose, prim mouth. He wore no facial hair, and was balding on top, a monk's fringe of black hair framing his head.

When he walked from the ladder to the bundle against the far wall, Paine saw the source of his gracelessness: one of his feet was turned out from the ankle at an odd angle, apparently broken and badly reset.

"Mr. Paine, I wanted you to see this," Tiny Man said. His voice was startlingly American inflected. He produced a small penknife, bent to the canvas-enclosed bundle on the floor, made a small incision at one end and ripped a line all the way down. He pulled the sack aside and there was the unmoving figure of Philly Ramos.

"Wake him up," Tiny Man said to the leader of the blacks, who immediately went over to Philly, bent, and began to slap his face. The blows had no effect at first. Then Philly seemed to swim out of the place he had been. He looked drugged. He focused on the black man standing over him and smiled.

"Poppa, how are you, man?"

Poppa hit him again, hard, with the flat of his palm across the face, and Philly's eyes became clearer and focused on Tiny Man.

"Jesus," he said. "Christ, man, you promised me."

"When I promise, sometimes I lie," Tiny Man said. He turned away from Philly as if he were of no further importance.

"Sit him up," he said to Poppa, and Poppa obliged, sitting

Philly up away from the wall and pulling the remains of the canvas bag away from him.

"Mr. Paine," Tiny Man said, "I want you to remember this, because this man did a wrong to you, but mainly because it will make an impression of what you have become involved in."

Tiny Man whirled toward Philly, at the same time lifting something from the inside of his baggy trousers.

Philly looked up at him and suddenly knew what was happening. He began to scream. Tiny Man's blade, which looked something like a long, not very wide, meat cleaver, came down and across, halfway cutting Philly's head from his neck. Philly's scream turned into a gurgle of blood, and the second swift fall of Tiny Man's blade finished the guillotining. He then proceeded, with fast, tautly muscled strokes, to detach Philly's limbs from his torso.

Paine tried to turn his head, but Poppa put his hands to either side of Paine's face and made him watch. One of the AK-47s pointed close by Paine's face, making him keep his eyes open. The dull, meaty sounds of Tiny Man's blade hacking at flesh were like nothing Paine had ever heard before.

It was over in a matter of minutes. Poppa released Paine's head and he turned to vomit, missing the dog bowl with urine in it, soiling the mattress. The fruit he had just eaten came up readily, followed by watery yellow bile.

When Paine straightened himself and opened his eyes, Philly's lifeless face was staring into his. Tiny Man held Philly's hair tightly in one hand, and he put this hand on Paine's head, gripping the hair, and brought the two heads close together.

"Would you like to say good-bye, Mr. Paine?" Tiny Man asked. "He will be fucking no more men, or killing any of my loyal workers."

Tiny Man yanked Philly's head away, threw it disdainfully into a far corner of the room, and went to the ladder.

He was about to climb up it when Paine said, "You killed Coleman, Johnson, and Quinones."

Tiny Man looked back at him in wonderment. "Of course. Did you think Bob Petty did those things? Petty has even more foolishness than honor. He has been following me for the past week, trying to do the same thing to me that I've been doing to his men. Johnson, he tried to hide, unsuccessfully. Coleman, he tried to warn, again unsuccessfully. I was even able to lure him away from Quinones for the half hour I needed."

Kwan had his foot on the ladder when Paine asked, "Why did you act now?"

"Because I knew Petty was coming for me."

"How did you know that?"

Kwan smiled and shook his head. "You are as foolish as your friend, Mr. Paine. I was told, of course."

"By who?"

"By someone in your government." Tiny Man smiled again. "We will see your friend Bob Petty soon, Mr. Paine. Bearing all of his foolishness and honor, he will come to save you." He began to scamper up the ladder, the three black men just behind him, one of them bearing the remaining fruit in its bowl.

"Perhaps," Tiny Man said, "I will let you say good-bye to him, too."

▽

29

AGAIN, PAINE WAITED. The heat lessened, and sometime during what must have been the night, he slept, and dreamed. And, for all that he had seen and been through, it was a peaceful dream.

Paine was on his hill, with his telescope, and he saw Bob Petty whole again. Though it might have been possible for him to do so, Petty had not gone mad. He had lost only his respect for himself, and had acted only out of love and honor.

And on his hilltop, with his telescope, Paine searched once more for Rebecca, who refused to appear to him. *"Maybe you'll think of me as holding you from now on,"* she had said. Paine wanted her to hold him now. But she was not there in the empty vacuum of space, and he cried out futilely to the scattered atoms of her dead body.

And then suddenly he was looking not into the eyepiece of the telescope but into its open end, and he saw his face huge in the mirror below. For now the instrument was pointed not at the stars but at himself, and he saw his own essential self, saw into his heart, and saw that Rebecca was there with him, had been with him all along. For the vast cosmos cannot compare to the human heart, which in the atoms of its memory breaks death and transcends time.

And he felt the memory of her arms around him, cradling his heart and protecting him from the cold night, and death was something he neither feared nor craved.

Maybe you'll think of me as holding you. . . .

And she held him till morning came, and he awoke into the air of another hot day.

Poppa and the others had taken the limbs and torso and head of Philly Ramos away. Paine was thankful for that. There were still bloodstains on the blue padding of the walls. Paine's water bowl had been refilled, and Paine drank half the water, and sat on the edge of his mattress, away from his dried vomitus, and tried to think.

His body was weak, and his mind. The ovenlike heat of the cellar told him to lie down and sleep, but he would not do that.

He looked, instead, at the half-full water bowl, and at the single light bulb in the center of the ceiling.

He picked up his water bowl, carried it to the corner of the room under the trapdoor in the ceiling, and put it down. Then he went back to his mattress, pulling it over beneath the light, folded it over, and stood on it. He was not high enough. He got off the mattress and folded it in thirds, making it three thicknesses high, and stood on it again.

It was just high enough for him to work at the fixture.

He pulled the insulation from around the metal box, finding the wires that led into the fixture box and tracing them away from it. He followed the line of the wire, which was stapled to the overhead beam, removing insulation along the way.

When he had a sufficient length, he found a spot where the thick electrical cable was bowed out slightly from the support beam and slipped his hand between beam and wire. He grasped the wire and yanked on it, working the staples from side to side until one of the tines pulled out of the wood and he was able to free the cable from it.

He worked his way back to the fixture box this way, yanking the cable and freeing it as he went.

When the cable had been freed from the last staple near the fixture box, Paine straightened out his mattress and moved it back to its original spot. He picked up his water bowl and placed it on the floor two paces from the wall under the trapdoor. Then he walked back to the cable, took a strong two-handed grip on it, and yanked it sharply out of the fixture box.

The basement went dark.

He felt up gently along the cable until he reached a spot near the end, where the cable insulation had been cut away to allow the individual wires to be separated, stripped, and attached to the light fixture.

Holding the cable at this point, keeping it well away from his body, Paine moved to the corner of the basement where the trapdoor in the ceiling was, trailing the cable behind him. He measured out two paces from the wall, found his water bowl, sat down on the floor near it, and waited.

Again, time was heat. Paine measured the day by the amount of heat in the cellar. In the dark, the game was even easier, and, for a while, it occupied Paine's mind. It was a better thing to think about than the way Tiny Man had hacked up Philly Ramos; better than thinking about what Tiny Man would do to him after there was no more need to have him around. Though he did not crave death, or fear it, he knew that it might arrive very soon. There was as little doubt in Paine's mind as in Kwan's that Bob Petty would come. The question, which was a question that covered most of the secrets of life, Paine thought, was when and how?

In the dark, as the day went along, when the heat had peaked, which put it somewhere around 3:00 P.M., Paine began a new game. Continuing to hold the cable carefully, switching it from one hand to the other when he got tired, he began to strain his ears for sounds from the rooms above.

At first he heard nothing. But he persisted. He thought of the way an astronomer uses averted vision, will look slightly to the side of an observed object because that part of the eye, away from the center of the pupil, is more sensitive to light and will see more detail. He began to use averted hearing, cocking his head slightly away from a barely perceived sound to sharpen his sense of it.

It was a bogus analogy, a mind game, but it worked. His hearing sharpened, and he began to hear sounds. A series of footfalls, a muffled exchange of conversation, a snatch of television from the far side of the house. He heard a door open and close; the volume of the television rose. Reruns of "Bonanza." He heard a commercial come on, someone laugh.

It took him hours, but he began to figure out their setup. There were two of them in the house. Two of them had left. He imagined that Poppa, with one of his cohorts, had driven in the jeep to the house on the Indian reservation. That was where they would meet Bob Petty. They knew Petty wouldn't agree to come where all four of them waited for him. They would hammer out a deal, and Petty would follow them back here. That was when they would try to take him. Tiny Man had enough confidence in his own abilities to be able to handle Petty alone; the others were mere insurance. Tiny Man also knew Bob Petty's mind as well as Paine did, and knew that he would do almost anything to get Paine freed.

Paine wondered if Poppa and his two friends were aware of the fact that they were nothing but bait. Again he heard a grunt of laughter from the TV room above. Apparently not.

The heat in the cellar diminished. Paine could almost hear night falling outside, rushing to meet his own imposed night.

The time when they had fed him the night before was already past; his body had tensed, and now weariness assaulted him with the realization that they were not going to bother to feed him. The television droned on—reruns of "The Patty Duke Show," "Laugh-In," "Dennis the Menace." He heard an occasional short blurt of laughter. The opening and closing of the refrigerator, a chair scraped across the floor. The front door opening and closing.

Finally, the television was turned off; the sound of night came to the house.

Then there was only the sound of one figure walking, from one end of the house to the other.

The walking continued for hours. Paine's back was painfully stiff. His legs ached, his eyes wanted to close. He was weak. He thought of the mattress, five yards away; it would feel like a bed of feathers to him. The walking above him was a susurrus, soothing him to sleep. He directed his averted hearing away from it, listening for other sounds, a creak of the house, night noises.

The night passed. Paine thought desperately of lively things, baseball games, boxing matches, raucous parties. His head drooped; he fought himself out of sleep, found he had dropped the cable. It had snaked away from him on the floor. He spent an anxious ten minutes crawling in careful arcs, until his fingers brushed across it, mere inches from the live wire ends.

He went back to his spot, measured two paces out from the wall, found the water bowl, sat, waited.

The walking above stopped.

With indirect hearing, Paine registered the clutching down of the returning jeep outside the house.

It was the coolest time in the cellar. Paine estimated that it must be an hour before dawn, the coldest time of desert night, a clean chill in the air. The sky above would be wide and pure, Saturn high overhead, bringing a preview of autumn stars up behind it in the east—Cassiopeia, the Andromeda galaxy, the Pleiades, peeking above the mountain horizon. An hour-long respite from the heat, the temporary banishment of summer.

Paine tensed, waited.

He heard no sound from above.

Then, he did. A door, not the front door, at the back of the house, thrown open, a tattoo of gunfire, a fumbled pause, more gunfire. Running. Something knocked over, a curse in the dark. Muffled shouts. More gunfire. A curse, followed by a single shot.

Silence.

Not silence. With his strained ears, Paine heard something, the stalking of a hunter, which grew to a resulting whisper. At the back of the house, four quick steps, followed by quiet.

So suddenly that it startled Paine, the trapdoor directly above him was yanked up.

Paine forced his voice to sound calm and faint. "What the hell's going on up there? The light bulb went out."

A quickly muttered curse, the metal ladder lowered into the hole.

A figure as small as a monkey scampered down the ladder.

Paine lifted the water bowl, pooled it around the bottom of the ladder, jammed the live wires against the nearest rung.

Tiny Man stepped into the water and screamed, a spark of light bursting around his small body. He was flung from the ladder, and Paine heard him hit the floor as darkness returned.

Paine threw himself at the spot where Tiny Man had hit. He missed by a foot, heard Kwan panting beside him, on his back. Paine covered him with his body, began to pummel him in the face and body, raining blows as fast as he could. Kwan's body was trembling slightly, as if electricity were still running through him, but Paine felt him stiffen, regain his strength.

As Paine reached for Kwan's neck, Tiny Man clamped his hands around Paine's wrists. His grip was steel. One hand left Paine's wrist and Paine felt it move down to a hardness at Kwan's midsection. The hardness moved. Paine took a hand from Tiny Man's throat, moving desperately around to Tiny Man's wrist. His fingers brushed the flat of hard steel. Tiny Man slashed upward, moving against Paine easily, and suddenly Paine lost his grip on the arm with the blade and he felt Tiny Man's arm move free of him, drawing back for a blow.

"Good-bye, Mr. Paine. I will cut you so that you will die slowly and no one can save you—"

Paine and Kwan were outlined in the circle of a flashlight beam as a shot split the air. Tiny Man grunted and bucked once under Paine, his eyes opening wide and then closing. Another shot and Tiny Man bucked and grunted again, less audibly. His knife clattered to the floor. It sounded as if he had taken a couple of punches, but Paine saw two red and growing stains in the side of his shirt.

Tiny Man's eyes unfocused and he went limp under Paine as Paine turned.

Bob Petty was standing at the bottom of the ladder, his police revolver still held in one straight, aiming arm. As Paine watched, Petty pumped a third shot into Kwan's dead body beneath him.

Petty's eyes met Paine's and locked there.

A long moment passed as the world reestablished itself.

Then Bobby smiled, a sad thing, and said, "Sorry I had to beat the shit out of you, Jack."

30

IN THE DESERT, IN the hour before dawn when the autumn constellations had not yet given way to the sun, Bobby Petty told Jack Paine what it was like.

"It's like nothing I've ever felt before, Jack. One moment my life was on a flat road, and I was traveling on a straight course. Then, with one bit of information, the road disappeared and there was nothing but hole in front of me. I remember looking into the TV room where Terry and the kids were watching something together, and when I saw her I felt dirty. I went into the bathroom, and looked at myself in the mirror, and it wasn't me anymore. It was someone else. A monster. I didn't even look at the girls. I was afraid they would be unclean if I even looked at them. So I went into the bedroom, and packed some things in a duffle, and said I'd go out for ice cream and took the duffle and left. I went to a bar up in Scarsdale, a noncop place, and I stayed in a motel room, and by the next morning I knew what to do.

"I went to the bank when it opened and took all the money out, and got on a plane for Texas. If I'd left the money Terry wouldn't have believed I was gone. I only had one thing in my head, Jack. To kill Kwan, and keep him from killing my men. The rest of it didn't seem important. My life was over anyway; the further I got from my life the better it would be. The only thing I wanted to do before the whole thing came out, before they lumped me in there with Calley and the rest of them, was to kill Tiny Man."

Paine had one question, but didn't want to interrupt. In

the purpling dawn light, he felt Bob Petty bursting next to him, wanting to spit all the poison out of him.

"So I followed him from Texas, back to New York." Petty laughed grimly. "I called that stupid bastard Coleman and told him Kwan was coming, and he panicked. I couldn't save any of them."

Petty stared at the horizon, looking for the sun that refused yet to rise. "In a way I think they were lucky, getting it over with."

This time, the silence was longer; the sun would not burst forth from the horizon, but Petty was looking beyond it, anyway.

"It was horrible in Cambodia, Jack," he said, his voice barely audible. "It was war, and I lived with it because of that, but face to face like that . . ." The whisper trailed off, returned, stronger. "It was something we thought we had to do, and we did it. For years I wished I had been in the air force because they got to do it from up in the clouds by pushing a button. It's no different, but they didn't have to look into the faces. There was one face I dreamed about for years. He couldn't have been more than nineteen. He looked into my eyes when I shot him. His eyes were the same as mine. Whatever happened, he thought he was doing the right thing. He was willing to die for it. That was my face. I knew that if that conviction wasn't in me, that if I wasn't absolutely sure that what I was doing was right, was saving the lives of my own people, then what I had done that day when that face had looked into mine and refused to look aside, was look in a mirror and that I had killed myself. . . ."

He was weeping, trembling beside Paine in the cool predawn desert. All of it came out of him, and suddenly Paine felt as if he were holding not a friend, not even a brother, but his own son. The bond was that close.

Petty wailed, "Oh, *God!*" and tried to bury himself, his memory, his very self, into Paine's chest, and Paine held him for a long time, and rocked him, and let the hurt flood out of him into the desert ground.

"Jesus, Jack," Bobby said, sitting up, pulling away from Paine. "Jesus."

And they watched, and still the sun would not rise.

"I have one question, Bobby," Paine said.

They looked for the unrising sun, and Petty said, "What is it?"

"Who told you that what you had done was wrong, and that Kwan was trying to kill off your unit?"

Bob Petty looked at him in the purpling light.

"I thought you would have known that. Didn't you talk to him? It was Chief Bryers."

Paine rose, and told Petty to follow. And, as they turned their backs on the cool desert, the sun, an orange beacon, thrust its lip up over the horizon, triumphant, promising light at last.

31

AT THE AIRPORT IN Tucson Paine made a call to Billy Rader, and one other call, and then they got on a plane. In the seat next to him, Bob Petty, exhausted, slept, but Paine couldn't sleep. He watched Bob Petty's fretful slumber, and he looked out the window and watched America move west under him, and after a long while he did sleep because the stewardess was waking them both, telling them with her vacant charm to fasten their safety belts because they were descending toward landing at La Guardia Airport.

They circled a few times, in a clear, blue, late-summer sky, with high, small, fat clouds that looked almost autumnal. The captain told them that it was eighty-nine degrees in New York, with a high expected of ninety-three, but that the heat was supposed to break that night. "If you believe it," he said, which made most of the passengers laugh, but Paine just looked at the skyscrapers below and waited for the plane to land.

When they reached the ground, as Paine had arranged, Bryers's car was waiting for them. Bryers got out himself from the back, without help from the driver, looking grim but satisfied. He smiled stoically and held out his hand for Paine to shake, saying, "Good work, Jack," but Paine ignored the hand and moved past him into the car.

Bob Petty sat between Bryers and Paine. The car trip up to Yonkers was strained. Bryers tried to talk a few times, but Paine looked out the window, watching New York go by. "You think perhaps we should have cuffed Petty?" Bryers said once, but Paine didn't respond.

By six o'clock they had reached Yonkers. Paine pushed out of the limousine as it reached the curb, and Bob Petty followed.

Billy Rader was waiting for them outside Bryers's office. There was a folder under his arm, and he smiled and rose to shake Paine's hand. Paine shook it, and said, "Thanks, Billy."

Rader's smile widened. "Wouldn't have missed it for the world."

Paine said, "Let's go," and they all went into Bryers's office, Bryers last, protesting.

"Shut up and come in," Paine said, and when Bryers was in the office Paine closed the door behind him.

"Go ahead, Bobby," Paine said, and Petty took a swing at Bryers and knocked him down.

"What—" Bryers started, but Paine said, "Shut up," and told Bryers to get up and sit in a chair. Billy Rader went around Bryers's desk and sat in his swivel chair, and Paine and Bob Petty stood.

"I take it you got it?" Paine asked Billy Rader.

"I told you my friend was pissed," Rader said. He opened the folder on Bryers's desk and drew out a sheaf of papers.

Bryers, nursing his jaw, looked from Rader to Paine. "You're all about ten seconds from arrest," he said.

"I don't think so." Billy Rader laughed, and then he consulted the papers in front of him. "Special Agent Kevin Bryers," Rader read, "covert domestic intelligence arm of the DEA, on loan for the National Security Council." He looked up, watching the color drain from Bryers's face, replaced by shock and anger.

"*How*—" Bryers began.

"Let me finish," Rader said, turning back to his paper. "On loan from DEA to the Yonkers Police Department, acting chief, on a twelve-month assignment to infiltrate, expose, and wipe out a Colombian drug operation just making inroads into Westchester County in New York. Said drug ring is already well established in Tucson, New Mexico, and

in southern California, and will use its connections in Westchester to move down into New York City and up into New
England."

"*I told you—*" Bryers sputtered. "*National security—*"

"I told you to let me finish," Billy Rader said. He consulted
his paper. "Bryers is the architect and chief administrator of
something called . . ." Rader peered close at the paper, then
looked for Bryers's reaction, "Operation TM." He looked up,
smiling. "I suppose that stands for Tiny Man. But what he's
really the head of is something called Operation Hush, which
even the dopes at the DEA who thought he was just looking
to shut down Tiny Man's drug business, didn't know about."

Bryers nearly fainted. "Oh, God."

"Your reaction is understandable, Acting Chief Bryers."
Billy was growing angry. "Because, let me tell you what a sick
crock of shit Operation Hush really is. I have," he said, going
through his papers to take out a single sheet, waiting for a
fresh reaction of despair from Bryers, "a faxed copy of the
original meeting transcript from tapes kept by Acting Chief
Bryers's secretary in Washington. She keeps everything, because she's smart, and isn't taking a fall for anybody. These
are Bryers's own words." He read from the sheet. " 'To mis-
represent, or shall we say, distort, Tiny Man's actions in
Vietnam, in particular the action of February 10, 1971, Covert Action Number Three-nineteen, excursion into Cambodia to eliminate supply depot. We know, of course, that
Kwan was dealing with these people, was doing drug deals
with them. I think we can use that fact, which, of course,
was unknown to the unit at that time. As far as they knew,
they were eliminating a hostile force, a major supplier to
troops using the Ho Chi Minh Trail.' "

Rader looked from Bryers to Bob Petty. "This part I want
you to listen to carefully, Bobby." He read from the transcript. " 'Which, of course, they were doing anyway. But Tiny
Man was playing it both ways, and I think we can make use
of that. Tiny Man's been having things his way for quite
some time. Special Forces knew that he was taking care of

his own business as well as ours when he took that unit into Cambodia. That village had been supplying guns and ammo to the Viet Cong, and cocaine to Tiny Man, and when they fucked him over on the coke he thought it would be a good way to teach a lesson so he told Special Forces about the village. They were only too happy to help him out.' "

Billy Rader grew angrier as he continued to read from the transcript. " 'But that was then, and this is now, gentlemen. We've been given a mandate to do something, anything, to clean up these covert operations, which could still prove embarrassing. I think that now we've got a golden opportunity to do it by getting Tiny Man, and that Special Forces unit, out of the way. And without dirtying our own hands directly, in the bargain.

" 'I've been studying up on this Special Forces unit, and I think if we turn them loose on Tiny Man, do a vengeance thing, tell them they went into Cambodia only to murder civilians for Tiny Man, they'll take care of Kwan for us. At the same time, we can tell Kwan they're after him. Turn the coin both ways, so to speak. At the very least, we end up with half the problem solved. We can clean up whatever's left, but with a little luck there'll be no dust at all. There's one man in particular, Robert Petty, who's got the background, the mental profile, to take care of things nicely. He's a cop in Yonkers, New York, and I think I can get in there myself, set the whole thing up. DEA will help me on that, they want Kwan bad themselves anyway. We won't tell them the rest, of course. Research tells me that—get this—Petty's been trying to bust up this drug operation from the inside before it gets established, and doesn't even know Tiny Man is involved. (Laughter.) Can you believe that? If I handle him right, it'll be like lighting a cherry bomb on the Fourth of July. (Laughter.) It's a golden opportunity.' "

Billy Rader looked up as Bob Petty took another swing at Bryers, knocking him off his chair. For a moment it looked as though Bryers wasn't going to get up, but Paine helped him back into the seat.

"And if you want my two cents' worth," Paine said to Bryers, "I liked the way you tried to keep me away by threatening me and then offering me a job."

"Here's the thing," Billy said to Bryers. "Your ass is cooked as of now, and you know it. I've got a man inside the White House who isn't afraid to blow his whistle. I've got four or five of your men, including your two DEA boys in Tucson named Sims and Martin, already lined up to say whatever I want to hear to save their own skins, especially after they heard how you used them and their agency. This thing makes Iran-Contra look like baby puke. And you know it. The American public never figured out that shit anyway, but they'll figure this one out real quick. I'm a good reporter and an excellent writer, and I'll make sure of it. Domestic spying, tinkering with government agencies, doing a Manchurian Candidate number on the head of a Vietnam War hero—shit, they might even lynch you. So the only choice you have is to spill your fucking guts to me before it gets to a House committee and the courts, and try to set the record in the best direction for yourself that you can." Billy took on the look of a prosecutor with the murder weapon, covered with the defendant's fingerprints, in his hand. "You're going to have to name names, and quick, shithead—or I promise to nail you to the cross."

There was quiet in the room. They could see Bryers running it all through the computer in his head. Accounts were being balanced, options weighed. They saw the tally go up, the shadows fall behind his eyes, the look of the caught animal, looking for whatever hole to crawl into, drop across his face.

"We'll talk," he said to Rader.

Billy's face lit up. He pulled a tape recorder from his briefcase and set it up in the center of Bryers's own desk. "Fine," he said. To Paine and Bob Petty, he said, "This may take some time, and I doubt you boys will want to hear all the grisly details right now. Maybe you'd like to go home, take a rest. The two of you look like shit, anyway. We can talk tomorrow, after I phone this in to the *Times Herald*. Be nice to see a Texas paper get a little glory for once " He turned a large, affectionate smile on Bob Petty. "When this is done, you're going to be quite a hero. I'll get a Pulitzer Prize, of course. Is there anything you want?"

Petty took a final swing at Bryers, hitting him squarely on the nose. Bryers doubled over, throwing both hands to his face, trying to stem the sudden flow of blood.

"Jesus, you broke it!" Bryers cried.

Petty said, "That's all I want."

"Go," Billy Rader said, and when Paine and Bob Petty left he was placing his microphone in front of Bryers, turning on his tape recorder, beaming like a six-year-old on Christmas morning.

32

I T WAS DARK WHEN Paine got to his office. There was no one laying for him in the alley, no one waiting in the hallway outside his door, only a new pile of bills and supermarket flyers inside the door, which he dropped straight into his wastebasket. There were no messages on the tape machine, but there was a long, thin manila envelope on his desk. Inside was his new lease, in triplicate, with all the changes he had insisted on. There was also a short note from Anapolos, apologizing for the delay, promising that he would never use his pass key again. The key was enclosed in the envelope. There was a new air conditioner in the window, the instruction booklet still on its string around one of the control knobs.

But the heat had broken. It had grown cool in the office, and Paine didn't need the new air conditioner. Anapolos's note ended by saying, "Have a nice day."

Have a nice day. Paine had had a nice day, but it hadn't been easy. He had gone with Bob Petty to his house, and he had watched, and smiled, while Bob Petty held his wife and his daughters as tight as a man can, telling them how sorry he was and what a fool he was and asking for their forgiveness. They had given it, of course. Terry had cried, so uncontrollably that for a while she'd had to leave the room, and later, after they had all talked until they were talked out, as Paine was leaving, Bobby had gone away, and Terry had taken Paine aside and kissed him and held him and cried again.

"There'll always be a special place for you in my heart, Jack," she had said.

Paine had smiled, and said, "Good, Terry," and then she had continued to hold him and said, "I'm not over you yet. I don't know if I want to be."

He had answered, remembering the way she had looked at Bobby when he'd come in, the fire that had leapt back into her from her supposedly closed, cold heart, "Yes, you do, Terry," and he had kissed her on the cheek and held her himself and then left.

Have a nice day.

Paine thought about driving upstate. He thought about the bass still in the pond behind his summer house, the summer books he had left unread, the iced tea he had left warming in its glass next to his chair in the shade, the telescope dome waiting to be opened to the night stars.

But he did not feel like looking at the stars for a while. He had found what he had searched for among them in his dreams, and found what he needed in his heart, holding him, at least for now.

And hot summer was over. Iced tea wouldn't taste the same; he no longer wanted to read the books piled next to his shade chair. With the breaking of the heat, shade would chill him. The bass would not jump so high from their cooling lake.

Have a nice day.

Leaning back in his chair, Paine put his feet on his desk, and waited for the phone to ring.